MW00476861

TONY

THE KNEEBREAKER

TONY
THE KNEEBREAKER

A NOVELLA BY ED GRUBER

To Vince
Buona Fortuna

Ed Gruber

DEEDS PUBLISHING | ATLANTA

Printed in the United States of America

Published by Deeds Publishing, Marietta, GA
www.deedspublishing.com

Cover art by Mark Babcock and Matt King

Library of Congress Cataloging-in-Publications Data is available on request.

ISBN 978-1-941165-47-8

Books are available in quantity for promotional or premium use. For information, write Deeds Publishing, PO Box 682212, Marietta, GA 30068 or info@ deedspublishing.com.

First edition, 2014

10 9 8 7 6 5 4 3 2 1

DEDICATED TO THE GRUBER BROTHERS.
THANKS FOR THE STORIES.

1.

TONY THE KNEEBREAKER FOUND GOD.

The Boys ain't happy.

"Joey," the big Italian-American galoot grumbled to Joey Lowenstein who, with brothers Ira and Freddie owns and runs the JIF Banana Trucking Company. "They won't let me out. Say I know too much. I won't never say nothin'. I'd be like a dummy. A clam. They should know I'm a standup guy. More'n twenny years I'm doin' things like they want, Joey, an' you don' wanna know summa what I done. But you're a smart guy. You been around. You probably already know good as anybody. After doin' all o' that for them they won't let me out. Tony the Kneebreaker ain't me no more. They don't understand God don't want me hurtin' no people no more—never again."

Looking back to the old days, there was Tony's name usually in small print—*very small print*, at the bottom of the fight card posters on display outside many of the Big Apple's boxing arenas—St. Nick's, Jamaica and Sunnyside Gardens, the Armory, and neighborhood gyms where the fixers and tricksters staged every kind of boxing match you can think of. From main events with big names to Golden Glovers, wild-swinging amateur wannabees, and shuffling has-been bums. Always SRO at the main arenas, and smaller but equally-as-vocal screaming-for-blood crowds at the local gym smokers.

What Tony was, was a ring rat—taking dives for up-and-comers out to build their reps, filling out the fight card in the prelims, earning sandwich money for getting his face scrambled. One look at that flattened nose he talks through, at the scar tissue that turns his still bright blue eyes into narrow slits, those cauliflower ears you wonder how he could hear through, and you know Tony was the outclassed patsy the sleazy mob-backed promoters (no less his boyhood chums turned gangsters), tossed into the ring too many times against too many other pugs for too little—too little for Tony. The sleazes and their backers, they made the killings while Tony was being butchered inside the ropes; a piece of meat, a punching bag, a means to some gonif's greedy end. And the end for Tony came sooner than he'd expected.

"I was never gonna be a contender," Tony continued, "just a—what do they call it, Joey, some pug showcasin' a comer, nothin' more. But I always gave it my best shot, Joey. Always a hunnert percent. I did okay, too; made a few bucks for myself an' for the longest time gave the crowd a good show. I had a good right an' could go a full ten without runnin' outta gas. An' I could take a punch; too many they said. I know I was slowing down. A lotta punches Joey, they begin to wear down the body, 'specially the fights I had to take a dump. That works against the head, too, an' you don't have the—I'm lookin' for a word, Joey."

"Enthusiasm?"

"Yeah, that's right—enthusiasm. You don't have it when you already know how the fight's gonna end even in the locker room, or they tell you just before you climb through the ropes an' it ain't your arm the ref's gonna lift up at the final bell. Never liked doin' it, but The Boys said it's what I had to do. Even those fights, I always did the best I could. Even without the—the enthusiasm, like you said."

Enough was enough The Boys finally agreed during one brutal bout Tony's legs were so full of rubber he could hardly get off his gore- and sweat-stained stool for the third round. "Fer chrissakes, the struntz' legs look like they're rejects from Firestone," they grumbled. "That slob ain't even putting on a good show no more. Get him outta there before we gotta haul him away on a stretcher, or call Grittani's funeral joint to send over the meat wagon."

Waste not want not. So The Boys, who were not only behind the fights, also took the book on them, and into a lot more dark and dirty enterprises, took Tony on as an enforcer for whenever some physicality was needed to pressure certain clientele. His primary occupation? Shuffling in to a business that was maybe behind in monthly protection payments. Or in front of a politician or city official who was unwisely, and without really thinking, re-thinking his arrangements with The Boys. Even facing up to a short-tempered, on-the-muscle longshoreman on one of the New York/New Jersey Port of Authority docks, Tony always got his point across. Standing in a welcher's doorway Tony was a big guy, a menacing figure. Every scared-stiff victim he stood face-to-face knew on the spot this was not going to be a good day. Those huge hands of his could still inflict heavy damage. One look at the scratched and nicked cut-down baseball bat tightly gripped in those massive and gnarled hands was often what turned things around—as a threat, or if that wasn't enough to do the job, strategically administered where it would hurt the

most and bring about a quick change of mind and heart...
and the inevitable envelope stuffed with cash.

When he wasn't being a bullyboy? To hang out otherwise on the docks where The Boys had their main action
and to do "whatever. " Still to be an immediate force to call
upon when the services of an intimidator were required,
which could happen more often than not on the volatile
docks. A lot of "whatever" included being Johnny-on-the-
spot to the various trucking companies and their drivers
as they needed him. It's The Boys' way of staying closer to
their "clients." Thus Tony's connection with the Lowenstein brothers and their JIF Banana Trucking Company.
What else was left for an ex-pug?

But, Tony the Kneebreaker, with his heart and still a
goodly portion of his brain intact, though with a modi-
cum of slurred speech and a face only a mother, his wife
Patty, and Tony Jr. could love, found God; at least some
degree of conscience, and a very powerful and passion-
ate feeling that God was not happy about his violent and
violating profession. So Tony was looking to go straight,
without too many places he could turn to get there.

"I got enough stashed away for little Tony's college."
he continued his confession to Joey, "If anything happened to me, enough Patty could pay bills an' more. We
ain't been big spenders. You know Patty, Joey. She's been
a sweetheart all these years an' all that time she was never
on me about my business. But I knew—you hadda know,
it ate her up inside. But The Boys, they took good care of
us. I mean even in the not-so-good times I always had a
job, an' it was hard to say no when they asked somethin',
not that they liked it if you did. They don' know from
'no.' They didn't give me too much choice. But now, now
God don't want me hurtin' people no more an' I gotta

think about gettin' inna heaven. I already been to hell an' put too many people through it with me. You gotta help me, Joey. You an' your brothers do business with 'em; you know The Boys good as anybody."

Joey Lowenstein knows The Boys very well. His first encounter, he was a fifteen-year old kid of the streets, wise beyond his years, and with chutzpah honed on the block. His mother's youngest brother Morrie, while the sweetest guy in the family, loved and doted on by all, happened also to be a very bad gambler—winning was not in his vocabulary or his ability. But he crazily never stopped trying. This time he was into The Boys for about four thou' he didn't have, and couldn't come up with on his own no matter how much time they gave him, which wasn't much on this particular go around. He came crying to his sister—Joey's mother, the family matriarch; if he didn't come up with the cash in forty-eight hours his arms and legs were in jeopardy, or worse they'd threatened. They weren't fooling around. Rachel Lowenstein, though annoyed with Morrie's immaturity and gambling addiction, and never shy of letting her feelings be known, was also a strong advocate of 'family.' When she finished bawling him out she was ready to do what she'd always done. Bail him out. "We're always here for each other," she'd often preach to Joey and his brothers and the rest of the clan. "Family comes first. That's the rule we Jews live by. No matter what."

"Oh, Morrie. these are not good times for everybody. I can't put all that cash together in forty-eight hours," she worrisomely sighed to her baby brother. "It's a lot of money and I have to talk to everybody in the family. We need at least another week or more to raise that kind of money. There's getting in touch with all the relatives and asking each to give what they can."

In spite of her disappointment in her irresponsible brother, there was no way she would allow Morrie to be victim of a savage beating from those gonifs, those thugs. Two wrongs don't make a right is the way she looked at it.

Joey, doing his homework in the next room, overheard the panicky conversation in the Lowenstein kitchen. Wise street kid that he was, he immediately thought of a way to help. Morrie, in spite of a bad habit of making bad bets with his local bookie with money he didn't have, did have the affection of all the kids in the family. After all, Morrie was like a kid himself.

One of Joey's classmates and schoolyard buddies was the son of neighborhood bookie Deefy Feldman who held "office" on the nearby corner where his clients laid bets with him seven days a week, rain or shine. Baseball. Football. Basketball. Hockey. The fights. The trotters and the flats. The dogs. Sunday morning pickup softball and handball games in the schoolyard just down the street. Even a cockroach race if somebody set one up. Deefy took book on any game anywhere, anytime, any amount. True to his nickname, he was seriously hard of hearing, but Deefy, reading lips like his eyes had ears, never missed a bet in his life.

Joey raced down the stairs of his building and over to the corner. Sure enough, Deefy was at his "office," leaning against the lamppost checking his betting slips. Joey articulated his plea, exaggerating the words in deference to Deefy's affliction, "Mr. Feldman, I'm Joey Lowenstein, a friend of Ritchie. You know me. Ritchie and me, we play ball in the schoolyard. And Morrie—Morrie Goldstein's my uncle. He's in bad trouble and they're gonna hurt him and my Momma's crying and trying to work it out with the family to pay what he owes, but they need more time. Can you help us?"

After getting all the details from a breathless Joey, Deefy said, "Relax Joey, gimme till tomorrow. Any friend of my Ritchie's a friend of mine. Don't worry kid, I got you covered."

Of course Deefy knew people who knew people who knew people, and he quickly arranged for Joey to meet the bad guys who held Morrie's paper.

Next thing you know, Joey, all of fifteen, is waiting nervously in front of his tenement to be picked up by The Boys, afraid his heart would pump right out of his body. They pulled up in a big black Buick. "You the Lowenstein kid?"

"Yeah," he managed to blurt out. "Joey, Joey Lowenstein."

They covered his eyes with a blindfold, and pushed him down to the back seat floor. His heart was going a mile a minute—maybe faster. It was a short drive—just a few blocks over to East Harlem that was the same crowded, rough and impoverished neighborhood like where Joey lived, only crammed with Italian American immigrants, mostly from Sicily. The car stopped in front of a walk-up tenement, the fire escapes up the front of the building serving as respite in hot weather, places to dry washed clothes, and too often as actual fire escapes. The driver and his associate got out of the Buick, opened the back door and led Joey up the front steps into the building. Did the gossiping and baby-sitting Italian-American mothers and grandmothers sitting on the stoop see a blindfolded teen being led up the steps and through the doors of the building by a pair of goons? Ask any them and each would swear on San Gennaro, the Patron Saint of Naples, " I never saw nuthin'."

The goons removed Joey's blindfold as they entered

the apartment hallway, making the sign of the cross as they passed a small pedestal on which sat a religious statue. They led Joey into the living room with the lampshades, stuffed chairs and couches all covered with stiff, clear plastic. A portrait of the Pope hung on the wall. You couldn't miss the Boss sitting in a huge upholstered chair in the middle of the living room, immaculate in a white linen suit, white-on-white shirt, white tie and white patent leather shoes. Fingernails beautifully manicured. Long black hair and a huge drooping mustache. An entourage of ethnic hoodlums stood and sat around the room.

"So what we got here?" the Boss asked the driver.

"This is the kid wants to talk about Morrie Goldstein, the Jew owes us four big ones plus the juice, on a paper we picked up from a bookie in the Bronx.

Morrie's bookie, Louie Aronowitz, with his "office" at the corner of 170th Street and Jerome Avenue up in the Bronx—under the IRT tracks, figuring he'd never collect the four-grand from Morrie, sold the paper to The Boys for two thousand. "A bird in the hand," he'd thought, happy to come out of a lose-lose with something better than nothing. The Boys? They'll make a quick and easy two big ones and more with one swing of a bat. More with the vig.

"The kid is family," said one of the goons, "the welcher's sister's kid."

"Your family send a boy to do a man's job, kid?" asked the Boss. "What do they call you?"

"Joey. Joey Lowenstein. They don't know I'm here," he managed to get out; his street smarts helping him to sense there was no hostility or threat to his wellbeing.

"You one gutsy kid. But you got one stupido uncle…

what makes you so smart when you got such a uncle, such a stupido?"

"He made a mistake, that's all. But he's still my uncle."

"So what you want?"

"We don't want Uncle Morrie to get hurt and we need more time."

"For what?"

"To get the money."

""Where you get it from? Rockefeller? Four-thousand's a lot of money."

"We know. That's why my Mom's gonna talk to the whole family. So everybody's chips in."

"See," the Boss said, turning to the henchmen, "Jews just like Italians. They got respect for family." To Joey, "How much time?"

"Probably a couple of weeks. Momma has to reach some of our people in Chicago. I think they're rich and they can help in a big way."

"All the way to Chicago, eh? Okay. You one gutsy kid. Okay. I give you three weeks. After that, your stupido Uncle Morrie gets a special visitor—my nephew Benny, who ain't such a generous guy like me and not as smart as you; he knows only to use his pugni—his fists, not his head."

"You mean it, mister?

"I say it, I mean it."

Thanks, mister. Thanks a million."

"Hey, like I say, you one gutsy, sharp kid. We could use somebody like you working with us. Make some good money. What you say?"

"Gee, mister. I ain't finished with school yet and my Mom would kill me if I didn't spend my extra time studying."

The Boss smiled. "You think fast on your feet too, kid. Maybe when you finish school you come talk to me."

"Sure. Sure, mister. I could do that. So it's three weeks?"

"Three weeks. That good for you?"

"Oh, one more thing, Mister."

"Now what?"

"The vig. What about the vig?"

"What do you know about the vig?"

From one of the goons, "He's a Jew…they know numbers."

"Let the kid talk. What about the vig?"

"We can't afford it. Gonna be tough even putting together the four thousand."

"Ahhh…okay. 'Cause you got so much balls, kid, we wipe out the vig. Just the four big ones. Three weeks. Okay with you?"

"Sure is. Thanks a lot, thanks mister. Can I go now? I gotta tell Momma the news."

"You go the same way you came. And you were never here. You don't know me. I don't know you. Not till you out of school. You get smarter, you bring that smart here."

"Yeah, I understand. I capeesh."

The only lesson Uncle Morrie learned from all of this was to eventually himself become a bookie, opening his own "office" in The Bronx at the corner of Morris Avenue and 167th Street, opposite Abe's Luncheonette. He didn't even do that well. Much to the family's consternation, embarrassment, and wasted lawyer's fees to which they all contributed, Morrie wound up doing three-to-five upstate.

That was Joey's first, and not last encounter with The Boys. He never searched them out…they just knew when and where to show up, like maggots.

Fact is, he and his brothers couldn't exist, no less be successful in the banana trucking business without The Boys. "With friends like these," the Lowenstein brothers wryly joked, "who needs enemies?"

"We'll keep things quiet around your business so you got nothing to do but focus on your business," The Boys promised the Lowensteins, "and you won't have to hire off-duty cops or guards or anything. With us, you spend a little money to save a lot of money...and you won't have no trouble. You'll get people cooperating you never dreamed. Your trucks'll get through where they're going— on time. Safe and sound. And your customers, they will be happy like monkeys in a ripe banana tree. It's what we do. Without us at your back you never know what could happen."

It's a peculiar insurance game that The Boys play; you pay them to protect you against them.

The banana business? It's one tough way to make a living, with a multitude of inherent risks throughout the banana growth and supply chain. From the unpredictability of Latin American and Caribbean politics to involvements with avaricious transnational corporations intent on keeping wages and social benefits low and volumes high. From the vulnerability of the fruit to pests and diseases to the dangers of pre-ripening throughout the transportation process. From the way packers and stevedores handle the delicate produce when storing down deep in the temperature-controlled holds of the reefers (refrigerated freighters) to when they're unloaded. And from how they're stacked in the trucks that haul them across America's roadways to wholesalers and retailers. With bananas, some kind of peril at all times, from the plantation to the palate. Not to mention The Boys and the shakedowns and the hazards of not cooperating which, in case of any kind of breach of contract, is usually destined—in this particular neighborhood, to include an ominous visit from Tony. Or in other jurisdictions, a Tony clone with the same persuasive skills. In any of the famiglia camps there's always a Tony. Or somebody worse.

When the banana distributors and wholesalers are placing orders and things are going well, JIF can tolerate the monthly payoffs. While the payments aren't small, they're not unbearable, and accordingly built into the cost of doing business. Mostly they've been good years for the Lowensteins, but it's a hard business—working the Hudson River docks year round—when it's hot, muggy and stifling, or cold, icy and bitter, shipping the fragile fruit interstate and across the Canadian border like the U.S. Post Office—neither rain nor sleet.

WWII veterans Freddie and Joey started the business about fifteen years ago, '48 or '49, after couple of difficult years of post-war hacking—driving taxicabs around Manhattan on the prowl for fares those lonely, scary and unpredictable night shifts. By day, the brothers free-lanced hawking fruits and vegetables at various neighborhood markets around the city from where the idea for the banana business took seed. When Freddie, a beribboned WWII Marine was recalled for active duty during the Korean War, brother Ira came on board to fill in, adding his financial and administrative knowhow. To honor the full brotherhood, they changed the company name from J&F Shipping to JIF Banana Trucking. It's been a very good living for the three brothers and their families. Seldom any troubles with the unions, the stevedores, the larger trucking company competitors, the gypsy truckers, contracts for the shipments, not even Port Authority management or the dock cops. Something comes up? The Boys take care of everything. You don't have to like how they do it or that they're into your pocket…only the results. If you don't like dealing with them? So what. It's the only game in town. No other choice. They got you right where they want you. But no one can say they're not willing, ready and eager to step in and get their hands dirty when they believe a lucrative partnership with a cooperating client is in jeopardy.

Like when Dapper Dominic, number two in command for The Boys, came into JIF's Newark Terminal office. "Joey," whispered Dominic, "let's do a walk-talk down the pier. Looks like there's a worry."

The pier? Part of the Port of Authority of New York and New Jersey that runs most of the region's transportation infrastructure, from seaports to bridges, tunnels, and airports. We're talking about controlling, or trying to control the largest seaport complex on the North American East Coast, at the hub of the most concentrated and affluent consumer market in the world—with immediate access to extensive rail network, and interstate highways—the very roads over which gypsy trucks (the drivers own their own rigs), haul JIF's banana loads

There's a ton of daily action on these bustling docks, with a bizarre cast of phantom and hands-on participants. The governors of the two states, a Board of Commissioners, the powerful corrupt unions, railways, and hundreds of transportation companies like JIF. And don't forget The Boys who make their well-paid living extorting regular payments from a long list of dock workers, their employers, freight company owners, the independent truckers colorfully and aptly called "gypsies," and anyone else who steps foot inside their territory expecting to make a dollar. Janitorial and security services. Electricians. Plumbers. Carpenters. Painters. Snow and trash removal businesses. Nearby bars and restaurants, pawn shops and check cashing joints. The tug boat captains. Even the shipping companies. You want a piece of the action? You pay. You want a trouble-free operation? You pay. That's the way it is and how it's been. And you can bet your paycheck—or your life—the way it's going to stay.

For the Lowenstein brothers, these docks are where, in freezing Atlantic Coast winters, hot and sweaty Hudson River summers, cussing, fussing, hard-drinking longshoremen unload the rusty banana boats tied up to the dock after long voyages up the east coast from Caribbean and Central American tropics. Plodding between the boats and the trucks lined up waiting to be loaded, stevedores of all shapes and sizes, every one of them mule-strong and some of them just as mean, lug the green bananas from down in the deep dark holds to the rigs, cooled or heated depending on the season and always maintaining 56-58 degrees temperatures. JIF's assorted fleet of gypsy trucks haul the un-ripened fruit—harvested green and hard, before they mature—points north, south and west. Their destinations; mostly wholesale banana distributors in metropolitan areas with their ultra-modern temperature controlled ripening rooms and packaging plants, mainly owned and operated by locals who either have connections or are themselves the connected. The Boys are everywhere. God bless America.

God bless Canada, too. There was the time Ira was making his first call on the Bommarito brothers at their ultra-modern banana processing plant outside Toronto in Mississauga. The New York Boys had suggested it'd be a good fit and arranged the meeting. Armed with success stories of satisfied customers, routings, potential ETA's, banana boat schedules, knowledge of the complicated red-tape ins and outs of border crossings, Ira was ready to sell Sal and Frankie Bommarito and their growing Ontario distribution network on using JIF as their primary supplier.

"You look familiar," Sal said to Ira, after the introductions. "Were you in the Canadian Army WW2?"

"I was Navy. U.S."

"I think I know where I know you; you do casinos, don't you? Gambling junkets?"

"Me? Nope. Never been on one or in one."

"The Caribbean? Havana? Nassau? How about these?"

"Uh uh. Nope. Never. Why? You guys like gambling?"

"Naah. Not the sucker side of the tables, anyways. Frankie and me, we used to manage them, and I could swear I saw you, or someone looks like you, at one of our casinos. Spittin' image."

Ira's antenna shot up. Casinos? The Caribbean? Management? He thought, "That all adds up to serious big-time Mafia...no doubt about it. Gotta watch my step with these guys."

It's been said that the Mafia were the experts on making profits at casinos, with expertise gained from Vegas, Reno, Florida, and other operations around the world. Buying off local government officials was the key to trouble-free operations—and while expensive outlays initially, these smooth, clever and ruthless professionals still came away with incredible profits. Oh yes, Ira was aware of casinos in the Caribbean. Plenty in the papers about Meyer Lansky, named by Senator Kefauver and his committee as one of the top ten racketeers in the U.S.

Among Lansky's boyhood friends was Bugsy Siegel, his partner in a bootlegging operation and who saved Meyer's life many times. Bugsy knew Lansky as Majer Suchowlinski, a Polish-Jew who had emigrated to the United States in 1911 when he was nine to join his father who'd moved here earlier and had settled in the Lower East Side of Manhattan. Lansky was a teenager when he met Bugsy, together eventually forming the Bugs and Meyer Mob that was known as one of the most violent Prohibition gangs.

His later associates came to know Lansky as the "Mob's Accountant," as he, along with Lucky Luciano—a notorious mobster, developed the National Crime Syndicate that ran a gambling empire from Saratoga, in upstate New York, to Miami and New Orleans, Council Bluffs and Las Vegas.

Interesting to note, although he was a Jew, it was reported that Lansky was heavily involved with the Italian Mafia in consolidating the criminal underworld.

This is the Meyer Lansky—invited by Cuba's President Batista to set up a legalized gambling venture in the hopes of doubling, even tripling the tourist flow. Lansky, with his organizational skills, imported a heavy support team; each man right near the top of the FBI's organized crime list. He named his brother Jake as floor manager in the Hotel Nacional casino. From Florida. to the Sans Soucie Hotel Casino, came numbers game genius Santo Trafficante—holding a full interest and other shares of the gambling commerce at the Comodoro and Capri Hotels. Joey Silesi became the business manager for Trafficante. Even tough-guy Hollywood actor George Raft was a part owner at the Capri. Plenty of The Boys from New York too, like Fat the Butch running the dice tables in the Capri. And bringing his special talents to the Nacional was Thomas

Jefferson McGinty of Cleveland's notorious underworld; another rare non-Italian.

This was all just in Cuba.

Although perpetual enemies of the FBI and Internal Revenue Service, The Mafia ironically had an arrangement during WWII to provide security for the warships that were being built along the docks in New York Harbor. With Nazi U-boats along the Atlantic Coast sinking allied shipping, there was was also fear of attack or sabotage by German infiltrators or sympathizers. So Lansky was instrumental in helping the Office of Naval Intelligence's "Operation Underworld" recruit criminals to watch out for submarine-borne and local saboteurs. Whatever action they had on the docks before the war, this arrangement was like giving the kids the keys to the candy store.

Only in America.

"No. No casinos." said Ira. "My wife and me, we're into the opera and Broadway shows."

"Well, from what the New York boys tell me about your organization," said Frankie, "we see no problem signing you on for the banana runs. But sometimes there's some business that has nothing to do with fruit. Things we like to cross the border with; both ways. Can you handle that kind of action?"

Once again the antenna; "If it's legit, we'll find a way to handle anything."

"Well, sometimes it may not be, as you Jews say, 'kosher…'"

"Is JIF getting your business dependent on us taking this on?"

"You know how it is, you do for us…" said Sal.

Frankie followed up with, "…and we do for you."

It was a long shot, but Ira felt he had no choice. "I'm

gonna level with you guys. And I hope you take it the right way. I appreciate the offer. Really. But it took my brothers and me a long time to establish JIF as a reliable and stick-within-the-rules company. That's why your friends in New York like and trust us and don't push us into deliveries we're not used to. And why we get no hassle from the law. I mean nobody bothers us. We're strictly banana haulers. That's all. That's what we do. And we're good at it. Just banana haulers. So we're not ready to branch out and jeopardize any of that. If you're looking for trucks to haul things more than bananas, that's not our line of work. But since you bring it up, I might be able to help. We know enough people in New York where I can maybe recommend somebody who may be willing to take on the risk and do as good a job as possible considering all…but it's not us. And we won't even look for a finder's fee. Compliments of the house. But not JIF. I'm sorry guys. So, if you don't mind, my brothers and me, we'd have to take a rain check on that."

"Hey, we appreciate your leveling. No offense taken. It's okay. Doesn't hurt to ask, right? Never hurts to ask. But there's one other thing."

"What's that?"

"We do everything on the books real legit, except for a little cash kickback for pocket money for me and Frankie. Like a percentage of the load. Any problem with that."

"We can handle that. Seems to be the way in the banana business."

"Okay. Since, you come highly recommended from New York, that's good enough. We don't even need to hear your pitch, right Frankie?"

"JIF is good in New York, they're good by me."

"So the deal's yours. You want to introduce us to your

other friends... have 'em contact us. But you change your mind about the other stuff...it'd be a nice little side business bringing in some big bucks. We're really careful. We know what we're doing. So maybe it'd be a little chancy, but we'd back you up all the way if you came on board. For now, we respect your decision. And we're looking forward to doing business."

It was a few weeks later the Royal Canadian Mounted Police found Frankie Bommarito curled up in the trunk of a Lincoln at the Toronto International Airport parking lot...with two bullets in the back of his head. Ira thanked his lucky stars for giving him the brains—and the chutzpah, not to get involved in that "other" side of Bommarito's business.

Like has been said, The Boys are everywhere.

Walking past the lined up trucks and the stevedores shouldering the green banana stems down the ramp from the hold of a just-docked freighter, Dapper Dominic and Joey Lowenstein reached the end of the pier on their "walk-talk." A practiced, furtive look left, right, all around, assured Dominic they were alone, no one was within earshot. You never know.

"Joey," he said, "we like you Lowenstein boys. You're like compares—good friends. Brothers. We got a nice arrangement going. You run a neat, clean operation. Know what I mean? Not to mention that stacked broad you got answering the phones. Mamma mia, ain't that Rosie something! But I digress. You invite us to your weddings and bar mitzvahs. You bring your families to our weddings and confirmations with classy gifts. Your wives are terrific ladies, and may I add each bella, very beautiful, and they get along nice with our women. You're okay Jews with a lot of moxie and a lot of class. Not to mention always on time with your monthlies. Never give us no troubles, and that's why you don't have no troubles. You know what I mean? Except, the word is out you are getting some grief from some mamalukes—some stupidos who ain't following the established system—people with greedy eyes, hands out. We do not like our associates being hassled. Puts out the wrong message that we ain't doing our job. That we ain't taking care of business. As you can surmise, we got a reputation we do not like seeing on the line. You know what I mean"

"Nothing we can't take care, of, Dominic," said Joey.

"No, no, no, Joey. You do not understand. My goombahs and me, we work hard to keep the docks workin' smooth. Everybody workin' together. Harmony, that's the name of the game, Joey. Harmony is what we like to see. People who cooperate. Respect the system. Don't make waves. You know what I mean? That's just good business. These docks? It's where we make a lot of our action. Puts the cibo—the meatballs and pasta on the table for our wives and kids, gives us nice warm cashmere coats like this nifty piece of merchandise I'm sporting, and lets us put some respectable wads of lettuce in the collection plate at the church Sunday mornings—we like to cover all the bases; you know how it is. What we do not like is our friends who help us make our living—we do not like them being put on or put out. You know what I mean?"

"It's not that serious a deal, Dominic. We're not being put out…"

"Joey, Joey…you know we always know what's going on. Even things we are not supposed to know, we know. We been around here for a long time; we got, uh, we got our fingers on the pulse as they say. So you gotta know we got connections. As a matter of fact, we got connections that has got connections. You know what I mean? So I'm gonna make it very plain and simple; we would like you to tell us who is giving you a hard time…"

What came next is what just about floored Joey.

"…and we will put them at the bottom of the river."

Joey swallowed hard. He knew The Boys know no limits to getting what they want. But this? This was an out and out offer to actually kill someone for him and his brothers. Took him a minute to partially recover from the shock of the offer. "No, Dominic, no—really. It's no big deal. We'll take care of it. If we can't, we know where you live."

"Okay. Okay. Have it your way, for now. We can respect that. Just remember; this river, it washes away a lot of troubles. So let us see how it plays out. We made the offer and it stands for as long as you need. As long as we're friends, the offer always stands. That's what we're here for, Joey. What friends do for each other. You know what I mean? So, we'll be in touch, like always…and tell Rosie I said hello, and maybe I'll see her around. That is some puttana you Lowenstein's got working the office, Joey. Some Broad. Momma mia! Ciao, buddy. Catch you later."

Yes, the Lowenstein brothers know The Boys well. And Joey knows that Tony the Kneebreaker asking to get out is like asking for either the impossible, or looking for trouble.

Tony continued, " You know I was a altar boy when I was a kid. Poured the holy water an' wine, lit the candles, rang the bells, carried the cross, an' the incense burner…I was a good Catholic kid. Every Sunday. When we got married, Patty an' me…we even had a church wedding, an' later little Tony was baptized. But all along I—it wasn't not believin' anymore, it was doin' what I was doin', doin' the muscle jobs, knowin' like it wasn't a good thing in God's eyes, but I was doin' it anyway, an' I was goin' to confession confessin' everything but the truth. Whatever I thought the Priest liked to hear, that's what I said. I lied to a Priest, Joey. To a Priest. On top of everything else I was doin', I wasn't tellin' the truth; I was a phony, a real babbo—to God."

"It's a hard world out there, Tony," Joey commiserated.

"Yeah, but it wasn't right, Joey. Wasn't right. Beatin' up on guys, shit, excuse the expression, but they had fami-lies…wives, kids, an' maybe it wasn't their fault they got in trouble. Things happen, you know. An' you shouldn't get beat up just 'cause things happen. There's always other ways out. Always. But they told me what to do an' I did it an' I kept my mouth shut an' they paid good an' I got respect, an' now that all ain't good enough. Like all what I did for them don't mean nothin' no more."

"I don't know how I can help you."

"Talk to them Joey. Have a sit down. They like you Lowenstein brothers. Maybe what you say would help make things better for me an' Patty an' little Tony. You got a lot of respect with them, Joey. They'd listen. Even what they do, they're really good Catholics. I know they'd listen to you."

Later, at JIF's office in the Terminal at the foot of the pier, "What are you crazy talking to Tony like that?" gasped Ira Lowenstein.

Ira's the youngest brother and financial genius of the family, learning office administration as a Navy clerk at the Portsmouth Navy Prison in New Hampshire during the war. Also, about growing and managing money as the personal secretary, before he was drafted and again soon after VJ-Day, to a shrewd and successful oil company executive in Manhattan who had become Ira's mentor. With Rosie's help, Ira runs the business part of the business—keeping the books—two sets, which is a juggling job on its own considering the illegal payoffs to The Boys, and the daily supplemental under-the-table cash handouts to union stewards, dock bosses, uniforms, kickbacks to customers, and anybody else on the take, of which there is a long endless list. There's also managing all the correspondence, licenses, contracts and paperwork, payroll, payables and receivables, investing the extras—profitably by last count. Ira had learned to be very good with money. Financially, the Lowenstein brothers and their families weren't hurting on a day-to-day basis, and with Ira keeping sharp tabs on their pool of investments, were building first-rate nest eggs for when the time was right.

"Those gonifs—goddamned thieves, they find out we're talking to him like that and you don't know what'll happen. But you can damned well expect it won't be nice. I'm talking about real tsores, deep shit trouble!"

"Easy," said middle brother Freddie, to everyone's surprise. Freddie's usually the hotheaded Lowenstein, thinking with his mouth and acting with his fists. There were times this served him well as a Marine Sergeant leading his platoon onto Pacific island beaches and through nightmarish jungle battles as they fought their way inland. And later in combat against the Chinese in Korea when he was recalled at the outbreak of that so-called "police action," and which all sometimes becomes too evident when he's handling the independent truckers—tough-minded freelancers that JIF contracts to haul the produce. But this? This was something could turn out downright nasty, jeopardizing the business they work so hard at—which meant it was important to keep their cool. Very, very calm and cool. "It's only talk. Nobody's doing anything, promising anything. I don't like this any more than you, Ira. But right now its just talk, right, Joey? Nothing more. Just talk? Right?"

Joey, the eldest, also an ex-GI, a superbly-trained Army Ranger and small arms specialist who survived the bloody landing at Normandy and the long gruesome grind to Berlin, spends most of his time on the docks. His job is making sure the trucks are loaded right and on time, checking each rig's heating and cooling systems to be sure they're set to the right temperatures; delivering frozen or pre-ripened bananas do not bring in the checks or keep customers.

"Hey," Joey informed his brothers, "I didn't say we'd help, or even what we could do. But you gotta admit, Tony—for us, he's been a champ. Whatever we ask, he gets done. Maybe his face got messed up inside the ropes, but his brain's a hundred per-center. And he doesn't make mistakes. Backs us up on the docks, cooling down the gypsy drivers when they get pushy. Helps me keep the stevies and dock foremen in line and makes sure the bananas get stacked right. And now that a lot of the fruit's starting to come in boxed, he'll help us with the gypsies re-rig their trucks. With Tony, our bananas always get where they're going on time, in good shape. Chicago, Detroit, K.C., Cleveland, Toronto. All those places our customers like doing business with JIF, and Tony's been one of the reasons. Not to mention the Italian goodies he brings from Patty's kitchen. I like he's kind of attached himself to us."

"We gotta be crazy getting mixed up in the middle of this. The Boys won't like it."

"We owe it to Tony."

"We owe nothing to Tony," griped Freddie, a little less cool than his initial inclination. "On top of what we pay those gonifs and everybody else, we take good care of Tony with a nice shmear. There's always a fat envelope for him the thirtieth of every month. He does for us. We do for him."

"Sounds like what The Boys say, "you do for us, we do for you." Ira added.

"We're not like them and never will be," challenged Joey. "They like when you begin to think and act like them—puts you right where they want you. Bad enough we have to deal with 'em. Dammit, I wish there was another way."

"No way around it," sighed Ira. "They may be goons, but they know more about our business than we do. Sometimes I wonder if they've got our company lawyer and our CPA in their pockets."

Are you kidding? One's our cousin and the other's a brother-in-law. Never happen."

"Oh yeah, wouldn't surprise me one bit. Those apes can be convincing—with or without Tony. But you can't say the way The Boys are connected in so many places that it don't work for us. Remember, they come with a lot of perks; they introduced us to some of our best customers all the way to Kansas City and Toronto. We never have problems getting licenses and permits; nobody hijacks our loads—maybe 'cause those road gonifs get better action with the TV sets, hi-fi's and fur coats they heist. Aside from with them behind us, nobody in their right mind'd think of hijacking a load of bananas—too much can go wrong with the fruit, considering the shmucks who hit the trucks probably wouldn't know a propane heater from an ice making machine. And where they gonna dump the fruit? Go into competition with the mob-connected wholesalers; some of them mob themselves? That would be like stepping in the lion's cage at the Bronx Zoo. You think they're gonna sell 'em on the street corner ten cents a pound? Don't be meshuganah. Moreover, we got first class parking spots for our cars, and the trucks waiting to be loaded. And don't forget we get priorities on the loading line. Try and do any of that without them. Not to mention the good deals we get on some of the other stuff coming off the boats allowed for spoilage or just lifted. I'm thinking those Russian sables our wives are wearing as examples. Out here a little mazel ain't good enough; you gotta feed the kitty."

"A necessary evil, I guess. But that ain't solving our problem with Tony."

"Since when did Tony's problem become ours?"

"Cut it out, Freddie. I know you don't mean that. Tony's like a fourth brother. He'd do anything for us. He loves our kids like his own and he'd do anything for any of us, including our wives. Anything."

"Then tell him to leave us out of it."

"Too late. We gotta help him and I think I know a way," said Joey.

"Yeah? What's it gonna cost us?"

"Nothing. We'll even come out ahead."

2.

A COUPLE OF DAYS LATER, AT JOEY'S INVITE, DAPPER DOMI-
nic was walking beside him toward the end of the pier.
A bitter icy wind coming off the river had both men
hunched over, collars up against the penetrating chill.
Days like this made you wonder how the longshoremen
handled it—some like the one they call the Mad Russian
with his leather wrist bands, studded belt, no shirt any
kind of weather, and shouldering those bananas, or whatever's being unloaded, day after day. Tough sonsabitches,
all of them.

"That problem," Dominic said as they stopped at the
end of the pier, and after he'd done his habitual look-
around, "the one you said you would take care of yourself…everything all square?"

"It's not a problem any more, Dominic."

"That's kinda like what we heard. Of course we'd o'
taken care of it for you—with pleasure. You know what I
mean? But that it's not a problem any more, that's the important thing. So something else must be on your mind,
Joey. Right? You got something you wanna talk about,
right?"

"Yeah. Right. Not a big thing, but you know how hard
it is—just my brothers and me, without no help. And you

can never trust the day hires to get it right a hundred percent of the time."

"An' you want to bring Tony on…"

"You guys…" sputtered Joey, who should not have been surprised.

"I told ya once Joey, I told ya twice…we know everything."

Gathering himself, "It just makes sense, Dominic. You know how dependable he's been for you. He'll be like that for us, too. We could use that around here. For your protection, he'll be on the pier, in the terminal, always around; we'll keep our eye on him, too. He won't be going nowhere, and he'll help lighten the load for my brothers and me, like he's been doing all along. The business is still growing, and we ain't getting any younger. There's a lot to handle. We take him on and make him legit being on a payroll, paying into social security and FICA, decent health care for his family, paying taxes—all legit; but you know what, he'll still be one of you, just doin' different kind of work. And you can't believe that—while it's none of my business, you can't believe he'd have his heart in what he does for you anymore if you didn't let him go."

"I'm gonna level with you, Joey. 'Cause I know you know things—you're from the street like me, so you ain't stupid. And I know you know how to keep your mouth shut. Like I said, you ain't stupid; you and your brothers. So, in the first place, Joey, we don't give a fuck about Tony's heart being in his work, as long as he gets it done right. You know what I mean? That goes for anybody in the organization. The job always comes first. Tony? He always got the job done. And he gets our respect for that. Getting out? That ain't an easy decision, Joey. He's on the books with us a long time and he ain't that punchy he forgets things, which would'a probably helped him some if he was. What we got going here ain't a North Jersey or Westchester country club where the high fliers buy in and get bought out anytime they get a sissy-ass feeling to move on. This is serious business…a lot of private business—very private he has seen and done that is our preference to keep in the family. Under the covers. Under the blanket. Under control. Our control. Know what I mean?"

"We're family aren't we, Dominic. Aren't the Lowenstein brothers kinda like family? Been vouched for year after year? And Tony's been true blue, hasn't he? Whatever you needed…I mean sure, we heard things. This is a small community. But he won't talk out of school, and you know me and my brothers won't."

"It's a good thing you won't. I mean that in a friendly way, Joey. Don't get me wrong. But when a guy gets religion, whatever…you never know. We don't need no gavones—no embarrassments. Ain't good for our reps. Bein' out does something to the loyalty factor. Kinda changes the point of view—the commitment, if you know what I mean. You never know what guys who get out gonna say or do. One confession to a goody two shoes priest who fuckin' forgets his vows and bingo, the shit hits the fan. And it's fongool on us. The cops or the Feds get wind he is out—they're always looking for an edge, and they put on the pressure like they know how to do. Who knows? One word out of line and bingo, like I said, the shit hits the fan. We don't like no shit hittin' no fan. Besides, one guy gets out, another wants out. Suddenly there's a run of guys wantin' out. Like a fuckin' landslide. We can't do business like that. You know what I mean?"

"Look Dominic. Tony really likes us and he wouldn't screw things up for us. We're people he trusts…"

"You saying he don't trust us?"

"Maybe not like he used to. Hell, look at how you guys don't trust him."

"He's giving us good fuckin' reason, Joey; not wantin' to stay with the family. But he has been a loyal soldier, I'll give him that…and maybe there is somethin'. Just maybe. Because he and me go back a long way and because it's you, I'll talk to him. Okay? Then I'll talk to Angelo, who won't be easy, Joey. You know he likes a tight-run organization. But I'll talk to him. No promises, Joey. Certain things we got to do our way. Capeesh? Know what I mean?"

"I capeesh. I understand. I know what you mean. Appreciate anything, Dominic. This could be good for all of us."

"Oh yeah, Joey, one more thing. With the D.A. and the Feds nosin' around these days, some kind of stupido crusade, probably lookin' for votes. Those finochios, they'll never learn. They'll never get rid of us. Like skin we cover everything. Anyway, there could be some knockin' on your door, some uniforms with papers, subpoenas an' questions. We expect you Lowensteins to be deaf, dumb an' blind. Know what I mean?"

"Sure. Right. Of course. We don't want to get involved. We just want to move bananas. Make a living. Nothing more."

"Tell Rosie I said hi. Ciao, buddy. Catch you later."

Rosie? This well-stacked beauty singled out Freddie in a Baltimore hotel bar while he was down there directing the unloading of freighters re-routed because of a New York union-manufactured slowdown on the local docks; something about dirty restroom facilities that was ultimately resolved when the union president's brother-in-law got the janitorial concession for one-and-a-half times the highest bid.

Not too many think of Baltimore as a major seaport. Or that it was an active port of entry and Naval base beginning 1670, and home to numerous shipbuilders for those multi-sail, speedy Baltimore Clippers that hobbyists make models of and put in bottles. Later Baltimore became a center for trade with the West Indies and China, and did a particularly lucrative business with South America.

Although Baltimore was a port long before it was a city, the State delayed its role in port development until 1827. Then, the Governor began annually to appoint State wharfingers who took charge of State-owned or leased docks, particularly those adjacent to the State Tobacco Warehouse.

With the Baltimore and Ohio Railroad connecting to Port warehouses at Locust Point in 1845, Baltimore became the commercial gateway to an expanding nation. As supply and demand grew for imported goods to Baltimore, ship production and design increased. The city was also a good backup when there was more ship traffic than the northern ports could handle, or labor problems like which brought Freddie to Baltimore where he met and flipped over Rosie. That was not to say he didn't love and care for his wife Fran and their sons, Ben and Sam. "I just got a lot of love to share," he'd privately boast, and as evidenced by his many quickies over the years. Rosie was different; she didn't just get under the covers, she got under his skin.

So Freddie brought her up from Baltimore, paid cash for a used cream-puff Ford Thunderbird convertible—red with imitation-leather seats, set her up in a garden apartment in Long Island City that was on his driving commute to and from the office and his home further out on the Island, and convinced his brothers she'd make an efficient, loyal and discreet secretary that they really did need. Their last hire spent more time on the phone with her whining, gin-soaked mother, and her unemployed leech of a boyfriend, than on the work overflowing her in-basket. "Besides," said Freddie about their former secretary, "she was not only ugly, she had breath like a sewer and shoulda been gargling more with a quart of Listerine. What'd she have for breakfast? Road kill?"

Moreover, Rosie also has a lot of love to share that she generously distributes among JIF's customers when they're in town, and also some of The Boys who can't keep their eyes off of her, or their hands. Rosie likes all the attention and keeps everybody happy in what Ira civilly calls "intimate public relations at its best." Not to mention she's a more than competent secretary, helping Ira keep the office business well organized and running like a Bulova.

Fran, though used to Freddie's sexual escapades, and understanding they were fleeting and never permanent, took special umbrage against her husband keeping a mistress—for her that was a totally unacceptable situation. Lucky for Rosie Fran never discovered who the babe was. But unlucky for Freddie and his brothers, Fran made some threats that were particularly fear provoking. These included a potentially hefty divorce settlement that could start with the sale of Freddie's beloved boat he'd named The Gefilte Fish, and go on to broadcasting to certain could-be-interested Federal parties about two sets of books and other troublesome such things. Needless to say, Freddie—recognizing a lose-lose state of affairs, did not require too much pressure from his brothers to overtly cut off the financial arrangements with Rosie, as well as the stopovers. Meaning that this gorgeous and seductive young woman was never without extra cash. And there were occasions, when the two were alone in the office, of a few kisses and touches and other things. Rosie does have her way. And Freddie does have his needs.

Rosie's extra-curricular activities, though unofficially sanctioned by the Lowenstein brothers are, "In no way," as Ira is quick to mention, "is it that we're pimping her for the company. What she does she does on her own, and while we do admit that it's good for the company and we sometimes slip her an extra few bucks for—let's call it 'her unique and special contributions to the organization,' we are not running a whorehouse."

Boiled down, Rosie does for them…and they do for her. Seems to be the way things are done around the docks.

In a quiet secluded corner of the Terminal, between ship arrivals, Dapper Dominic sat with Tony on a pair of empty crates. It was much too cold this bitter New Jersey day to do a walk-talk down the pier.

"How many years we know each other, Tony? Huh? Since we were kids playin' stickball on the street. Hangin' at Sabatini's candy store. Liftin' pennies off the newsstands. Runnin' errands for Fat Frankie when he bossed The Boys. Roastin' mickeys in a fire over at the empty lot between your buildin' an' mine. Gettin' chased around the block by the fuzz for whatever. You. Me. Frankie One Punch. Eddie Lump Lump. Beansey. Rocco the Socko. Didn't we all used to go to your fights? Remember? All our street compares, all your pals, now all of us together, part of the family. True to the family. Your family. You know what I mean? So why all of a sudden God pops up to change everything. You been goin' to church all your life and crackin' knees more'n half your life. So what's the deal?"

"Look, it ain't like I heard a voice or anythin' like that. I may be a big, dumb pug, but I know enough God don't talk to people, not even the Pope, may he live a long life. But people talk to God, an' it's like gettin' things off your chest. You know, like when you're hurtin' from when your Mother an' the old man got sick an' died. Or your kid gets hurt playin' ball in the schoolyard. Or when I married Patty knowin' what kind of work I did tryin' to figure about bringin' her in my life with all of that goin' on. So, all along I talk to God about these kinds o' things an' it helps to clear your head an' get to where you know what you gotta do next. God kinda helps you get things lined up so you take the next steps with things make sense. This next step? The idea of gettin' out? It started when I was punchin' out that guy from Staten Island—you remember, the mamaluke was hittin' on some of our bag boys an' tryin' to get in their pockets, an' then cryin' when he sees the Louisville that he promises to go straight an' even leave the city, take his girlfriend an' their kid an' move to Chicago or somewhere, and I'm thinkin' his whole life is changin' 'cause of what I'm doin' to him an' I don't even know who the hell he is; just that he done the family wrong. He got greedy an' made a mistake an' he's settin' a bad example an' don't know what's gonna happen the rest of his life which, if I don't do my job right, could be a very short one. But I stop hittin' on him an' I tell him to pack his bags an' start travelin', that I don't want to see him no more. An' when he's gone I begin to cry; first time I cry since little Tony was born, but a different kind of cryin', an' finally knowin' what I been doin'—first time ever ownin' up to my job as what it really was, an' I got thinkin' that this is not what God put me on this earth—to hurt people. I seen that I was even hurtin' Patty, 'cause she was bein' forced to buy in what I was doin' 'cause I didn't give her much choice. An' little Tony? He never knew an' still don't, but what I tell him I just work the docks as a kind of foreman—an' I know all along I'm lyin' to him, to my own kid—my own flesh and blood, 'cause when we talk about it I get sick right here in my gut. Like somebody came in with a haymaker or a rabbit punch or somethin'. An' all this was comin' out like sewer water outta the pipe inna the river an' my mouth tastin' like when you drink sour milk. That's when I figured no more. No more. This ain't what God wants from people—he wants them to make choices where they don't hurt nobody, where they make an honest livin', don't lie to each other. Or to themselves. So it ain't religion or the church that's new for me. None of that altar stuff—it's livin' the way the priests talk about, but that what you don't see too much these days. All the rest is baloney—God listens while you talk an' while you talk the funny thing is you get your own answers. I know that now. You ask what's the deal? Best I know, that's the deal. Maybe you don't see it like I see it, Dominic, but that's it. That's the deal."

"Okay, Tony. I capeesh. Because we go back, all I can do is talk to Angelo. To be honest, even he loves you like a brother I do not think it looks good. You're makin' a big mistake. What you're askin' is pushin' too hard. You put your hands—and the bat, on too many marks. You know what I mean? Too many years. Too many memories. Too many swings with the lumber. Too many scars. You got a history with us that ain't easy to toss away and forget. No, I do not think it looks fuckin' good. But that's only my personal opinion, for what it's worth. Know what I mean?"

3.

WHEN THEY WERE YOUNG AND WEREN'T COMMITTING PET-
ty, or even major crimes, Tony, Angelo, Dominic and the
rest had another life. That part where they were just kids
hanging out on the corner in front of Sabatini's—the
ubiquitous New York City candy store, forging lifelong
friendships and in their cases, criminal alliances.

A wooden newspaper stand out front where customers,
rushing to the subway station, the bus or trolley car stop,
on their ways to their jobs, dropped off their pennies as
they picked up a New York Daily News or The Mirror
or the Post. The weather-beaten striped awning Fiorello
Sabatini unwound every morning at 6:00 A.M. to protect
the newspapers and shade the windows. Inside, a marble
counter, a few ice cream parlor wire chairs and marble-top
tables, a couple of booths, a Canada Dry ice box—with
real ice, crammed with bottles of Pepsi, Coke, orange, gin-
gerale and chocolate sodas, ice cream pops and cups of
fruity ices. A glassed-in candy bar and chewing gum display. On the walls, advertising posters for bottled sodas,
Bryer's ice cream, and cigarette brands, and some shelves
with boxes of cheap toys and board games for sale. Behind
the counter, the soda fountain and the cigar and cigarette
rack. Sabatini had his own rules about selling smokes to
underage kids. He wouldn't sell them if you weren't a

teenager, and he thought nothing of opening a pack and selling "singles," one cigarette—a Federal and State no-no—and a wooden match, for a penny. There was the Ma Bell phone booth inside the store that served much of the block; most families didn't have their own phones then, and when there was a call, one of the kids hanging outside was dispatched to race down the street, up the stairs, ring the doorbell and call out, "telephone fer ya at Sabatini's."

Sabatini opened every morning at six, seven days a week. After untying the newspaper bundles dropped off in the early morning hours by the delivery trucks, and sorting them out on the stand, he'd go back inside to prepare the tuna fish and egg salads for the noontime sandwich business. Carmen, his wife, she'd come out at eleven—they lived in the back rooms behind the store, to relieve her husband who'd sack out for a few hours, then return later so she could move to the back to prepare dinner for the family, supervise Silvio, Sergio and Christina's homework, and listen to the old Philco radio while performing the never-ending household chores. Around ten, Fiorello would clean up, mop up and close up.

Wintertime, as long as the kids hanging out bought a soda or a candy bar and weren't making trouble, Sabatini allowed them to stay inside. He enjoyed their banter and laughter. Good weather days they congregated outside where the guys paid a lot of attention to the neighborhood girls sashaying by—sometimes sashaying by more than once.

"Hey Angelina, did the bumps come with your sweater?"

"No. Did your balls come with your pants?"

"Ooooh, Serafina, ya look hot tonight. Wanna go to the alley wit' me?"

"I would, but there's no room there. It's where yer father's doin' yer sister."

The gang's teenage innocence and repartee at the corner took on new and nasty significance when Angelo, Dominic and the rest huddled together to plot their disreputable comings and goings. It was also where local mob boss Fat Frankie would recruit his pick of the lot for running errands and other illicit and sometimes violent tasks…introducing these already-not-so-innocents to the big-time and whetting their appetites for easy money and thrills. Fat Frankie'd drive up in his big Packard and the kids would gather around. Strutting, vying for the big shot's felonious-intended attention. The candy store and the corner? For some, a grand growing up experience. For these future gangsters—a training ground for evil.

4.

IT CAME THAT TIME FOR A MAJOR SIT-DOWN WITH TONY. Angelo chose the familiar and accommodating La Columba Italia Gardens across from the old Brooklyn Navy Yard. Out of the way, yet an always-bustling establishment with diners lining up Friday and Saturday nights, La Columba, with the typical Italian restaurant menu running six pages, is most famous for its Lobster Fra Diablo. Fresh lobster cooked in a noisy, steam, smoke and exotic aroma-filled (mostly garlic and oregano) open kitchen, and served at community tables featuring former milk bottles brimful of homemade grappa that, at the end of the meal, the patrons inform the waiters how many glasses they'd filled and drank. Popular too, among select clientele as The Boys, for its back room with a private entrance off the alley; a quiet and secluded setting for special meetings like this one with Tony as guest of honor.

"Sit down, Tony. Have a glass of vino. Gonna be a long night."

"Thanks, but you know I don't drink," Tony responded to Angelo D'Allessandro's sociable, yet foreboding offer.

Angelo D'Allessandro? You don't let how Hollywood good-looking he is—in a more mature Vic Damone kind of way (before the nose job), make you forget how focused he could be on the business at hand. Or how life or death decisions come as easily as a wave of a hand or a nod to an always-nearby soldier. Managing this local brotherhood is his business and he does it well; always cool, always in control, always methodical, ever prepared to resolve a problem with kid gloves or brass knuckles or the threat of a bullet in the back of your head…or the actual bullet. Whatever gets the job done. Whatever feeds the family. Whatever protects the family. Whatever prolongs the family. Always cool. Except when he loses it.

"Oh yeah, I forgot. That's a good thing. Especially in your kind of work; got to keep a clear head, right?"

"Right, an' my work is what I want to talk about…"

"Plenty of time for that, Tony. Right guys?" D'Allessandro addressed the other goombahs seated around a table covered with the traditional red and white checkered tablecloth, with a wooden bowl brimful of still-warm Italian crusty bread, a cruet of golden olive oil, and a bottle half-full of grappa you could still smell the earth the grapes were grown in. "We gonna eat first. I ordered lobster and pasta agrio et olio for everybody. Specialty of the house. Okay?"

Nods and grunts. Whatever the boss says—about anything. Especially when it comes to buon cibo—good food.

"So Tony, how's Patty and Little Tony? The kid still going to that parochial school in Queens? Best place for a good Catholic kid. Learn his catechisms, maybe become an alter boy like his old man was, eh? And I hear he's the stickball star on the block. Maybe play for the Yankees some day, eh? Be another DiMaggio."

"If that's what he wants," answered a worried Tony, who wished they'd get on with the issue and stop the baloney—which wasn't their style. They liked to feel out their prey, test nerves, observe their adversary's demeanor; like a cobra weaving before its quarry.

"Never know with kids these days," chimed in Dapper Dominic. "My Sal? One day its baseball and the next it's basketball. One day it's Pepsi, the next day it's Dr. Pepper, the next day its egg creams. Kids do not know what they want these days. Know what I mean? When they do, they got minds of their own. My old man woulda put the strap to me. But as long as they're good kids, listen at home, stay outta trouble—or hey, not get caught," which raised laughs around the table, "and go to church on Sunday, what more is there?"

From Gino the Grip, legendary for a chokehold that could go either way, resulting in a victim who accedes to Gino's wish of the moment, or a victim who becomes a corpse, "I'm lucky Francesca and me ain't got no kids. These are crazy times to bring 'em up. Too many wars in places I can't even pronounce their names they could get caught up in…people getting killed all over for what? What the fuck is this world coming to?"

"Always been that way, right Tony?"

"Yeah, I think so. Maybe we could talk…"

"Ahhh, here's the lobster," announced D'Allessandro as the waiter entered carrying a large tray of Lobster Fra Diablo dishes and bowls of pasta shiny from the olive oil and pungent from the sautéed garlic bits. "Ever watched the cooks out there making this stuff?" asked Angelo? "Splittin' the lobsters right down the middle, taking out the stomach up near the head, frying the halves in hot olive oil in those iron pans full of a ton of chopped garlic, sprinkle some oregano and basil and hot pepper flakes—especially the pepper flakes, can't have enough fire for me. Pour in a little vino— maybe more than a little, eh? Tomatoes, clam juice, steam it some…mamma mia, and laying it all down on some al dente linguine. You guys are gonna love this. I had these lobsters brought in special, just for tonight. Big ones for big paisano appetites. And for you," he turned to Eddie Lump Lump, "I ordered two. Mange. Mange. Enjoy."

Tony didn't. He couldn't. Everything tasted sour, or was it the bile racing up from his stomach? What were they setting him up for and why is it taking so long? He pretended to eat, taking small nibbles. Another time, another place he'd be doing the foonah, dipping the bread in the juices on the platter, and finishing every last bit of the luscious white lobster meat and the pasta. Not tonight. He had no appetite. For the food—or the small talk.

And there was lots of small talk; football, basketball, boxing, who's doing what from the old neighborhood. Even, who's doing who. And wheels.

"Still got that Super 88, Vinnie?" Angelo turned to Eddie Lump Lump. "What, a '56, right? Two hundred forty horses under the hood! Mamma mia!"

"Yeah, a '56. 324-cubic inch with 240. Best Oldsmobile ever outta Detroit, 'cept the carb's acting funny lately."

"So get it fixed."

"Ain't that easy. I went to Mauriello at the garage and he says it's better to take it to a Olds' mechanic, but the dealer where I brung it, he won't fix it."

"Whaddya mean he won't fix it?"

"The sonabitch says I never give him my right name and address, so he don't want me comin' back. Said I should go where I bought it.

"So take it where you bought it."

"I did. They won't fix it, too. Gimme the same reason."

"What are you doing tomorrow?" asked Angelo.

"Not much. The rounds, shaking some hands, and picking up a few late collections."

"You call me when you finish and we'll take your Olds

to the dealer from where you bought it and we will drive that beautiful Super 88 Oldsmobile of yours right into that greasy garage and he will fix it."

"He already said he wouldn't," whined Eddie.

Angelo, like ice, "*Eddie, we will put a lead pipe between his eyes...and he will fix it.*"

End of problem!

The dinner plates piled with leftover red lobster shells, the waiter reentered and was removing the dishes. D'Allesandro, with no shortage of flash, tucked a c-note in the old waiter's apron pocket, "This is for you, goombah, don't spend it all in one place. And tell Vinnie," referring to La Columba's owner, "tonight was the best ever. A nice farewell to our good friend Tony."

Tony's eyes went wide. What'd he mean "farewell?"

"So, let's get down to business." Angelo sat back in his chair. "Tony's been talking about wanting out, and he's got his reasons. Tony, I know you had a little talk with Dominic and he explained everything to me as he got it. But you know me. I like to hear it straight from the horse's mouth. How about it? What do you want to do this for? Huh? We're your compares! Not just your friends. Like brothers. We go back a long way. The corner. The block. The fights. The church. Our business. We're family. We got history. A long history."

"I didn't think nobody'd mind after all these years. You know I wouldn't never say nothin'. I'd never forget Omerta—the code of silence. Never. You guys been real good to me an' I done all you ever asked, and more. Beginnin' with my time in the ring. I built up all your respect, didn't I? So I didn't see no problem with me getting out an' doin' somethin' wouldn't be a sin in God's eyes any more."

"I don't know about what you did being a sin. Some

things have to be done. That's the way it is. It's taking care of business, Tony. Just business. Always business. God's a businessman, even he capeeshes. The main thing is, you get out you don't associate with your friends no more. You make new friends who don't understand us and the way we do things. Or where you come from. We don't see you. You don't see us. Not being connected no more, how do we know you don't say the wrong thing some time? How do we know you ain't gonna say anything? Ain't gonna flip? People get careless. The law brings down pressure. Mistakes happen when you're not tight with your family."

"Twenny years, Angelo, twenny years I never said nothin' about who, when or what. Not so much even to Patty, though she could guess things. She's no dummy, you know. You know I wouldn't do nothin' to hurt Patty or little Tony. Or my compares. I'll always be family, always. Just movin' over a little, you know. Just movin' over an' payin' more attention to God and what he wants from me."

"And you'd be working with the Lowensteins?"

"Sure, the Lowensteins. Good people. Never far away… right there in the terminal, on the docks, in their office, or at the house in Queens with Patty an' little Tony, all where you can clock me 24/7. The Lowenstein brothers? You never have no troubles with them. They like me an' I like them an' they said they'd take care o' me while I help 'em out. They like what I do for them. I like doin' it. kinda like a mutual business arrangement. Ahhh Angelo, I just don't wanna hurt nobody no more."

"You know you're hurting us by leaving. We always counted on you and you always got the job done. No questions. No look-backs. You always took care of business. One job at a time, time after time. Always very dependable. Reliable. Loyal. Always a good soldier. Always good results. A real professional!"

"Yeah, I know. I never thought o' doing nothin' else; nothin' else I could do. An ugly bum like me knows only how to use his hands. But Joey an' Freddie an' Ira, they say I could be a real help to them at JIF, an' I know I could. An' it'd make Patty happy 'cause now she don't want me doin' bad things no more an' you know I'd die for her."

"Was a time you'd die for the famiglia."

"Sure. It was part of the deal. Was always a chance of that happenin'. But I got lucky—maybe God was lookin' out for me, an' here I am now, me, lookin' out for me!"

"Here we all are," sighed D'Allessandro. "Here we all are with a tough decision to make. A very difficult decision. You making it very hard on us."

"Can't be that hard," Tony offered. "I'm like a clam, mouth shut all the time."

"We gotta be sure of that Tony. That's why we come up with a deal for you."

"A deal? What kinda deal?"

"One last job."

"An' after that?"

"After that it's okay with us you go over to the Lowensteins. But we're always in touch. We want to know where you are, when you are, how you are, what you're eating, drinking, smoking, when you're taking a dump, who your friends are. Got a problem with that?

"Who do I beat up?"

"No beating. This is a big one. What'd that Nazi prick Hitler call it, fellas? Oh yeah, a final solution."

"Final solution?"

"Yeah."

"You mean a whack job?"

"That's it. You get to take somebody out. And then you're out!"

"Drop somebody? I ain't never done nothin' like that. A few punches here an' there, some slappin' around, an' a couple taps with the Louisville…but I ain't never killed nobody. 'Cept that one time in the ring. You remember that. You all remember that. You was all there that night. But that kid had a bad heart nobody knew. He never shoulda been inside the ropes."

"Yeah, that was a tough deal. Not your fault. No way, Tony. Tough break for the kid. You remember, we sent flowers. But this'd be okay. We're talking about a nobody. A low life bookie—Sammy the Spic, who's a skimmer. You know him. You already put the lumber to his knees a couple of times, but he's a slow learner and he's still peeling off the top. Goddam thief! We got to set an example."

"Why not Gino, here? Or Ralphie. Or Eddie. Somebody done that kind of work before?"

"Because we want you to do it. Because we want you to know that if you take any of us down, you go down too."

"Angelo. Angelo. You can't mean that. I ain't never takin' nobody down. I ain't a rat. I already told you a hunnerd times—like a clam."

"Yeah, but if we got pictures of you doing a hit, then we know for sure you ain't gonna rat. For sure you'd get the hot seat and you don't want Patty being a widow and little Tony being without no father rest of his life to go to his ball games."

"You really want me to do somebody?"

"Your hearing's still good."

"An' you're gonna take pictures o' me doin' it?"

"You got the picture. But not me. I don't know shit

from cameras. Nobody here either. We're talking about Lowenstein. Joey. The brother always shooting pictures around the terminal and the dock with that German camera."

"This ain't good, Angelo. This ain't right. Joey's got nothin' to do with this. An' me knockin' somebody off? It ain't right."

"Leaving the family ain't right, either. But this is the way it is."

"I don't know, Angelo. I don't know. This is somethin' I gotta think about. Oh yeah, somethin' I really gotta think about."

"Sure. Take a couple of days. That little fuckup Sammy ain't going nowhere. Not while he thinks he's got some skimming left."

"Angelo, Angelo, I can't believe you guys come up with this."

"You been around, Tony. You know the score. We do what we have to do. Just protecting the business. That's all. Hey, remember, you're the goombah started this. So go ahead, think about it. Take all the time you need. I'll tell you what, take till next week. We'll finish everything next week. We don't want to be difficult to deal with. Not with a paisan. You want out? You do the hit. You don't do the hit? You stay and do what you do best. Either way, everybody'll be happy. Tell us next week, okay? And tell Vinnie on your way out give you some takeout for Patty and the kid. Anything you want. It's on me. Next week, Tony. And remember, only two ways to go. This way and the other. That's the way it is. Strictly business. Capeesh?"

A confused and distressed Tony nodded as he rose on those same kinds of rubbery legs that got him out of the fight game twenty years ago. Eager for some kind of support, he looked over to Dominic—who only shrugged. Somehow, through his disbelief and disappointment, Tony managed to say, "Capeesh. Strictly business."

5.

"OH TONY," CRIED PATTY, AFTER TONY HAD RELATED THE mob boss's outrageous offer, "maybe we should have let well enough alone. Maybe I should never have said anything."

They sat in the kitchen that, as in most other ethnic New York City homes and apartments, was where every bit of family business took place. Meals were planned, cooked and eaten, budgets made and bills paid, the little radio blaring soap operas, kids doing their homework, families making every day, as well as life and death decisions—like this one.

"Not your fault, Patty. It's all on me. A big dumb punch-drunk who shoulda been happy luggin' bananas with the other stevies, or drivin' a truck. But these were guys I grew up with, there was good money coming in, an' it was all I knew how to do. I couldn't fight no more. Just another pug couldn't figure out something good to do with his life an' got himself in some stupid mess."

"Don't, please don't put yourself down. You have more smarts and more heart than those galoots'll ever have. Any of them. They use people. Just use people and throw them away when they're done. And they make a big show of believing in Jesus and God and being good Catholics. God should strike them dead. I mean it, Tony. A lightning bolt should send them all to hell. Oh Tony, maybe we should forget it and just go on like we've been."

"No. No, no, no. Too late for that. It'll never be the same now. They'll never look at me the same again. I'm marked. It's time. Time to get out. I just don't know how."

"What about if we talk to the Priest?"

"Won't change nothin'. Who you think puts up the cash for the lights and the heat in the church, an' keeps the priests in their nice wines and fat cigars? The Boys drop big money inna box every Sunday; no Priest is gonna give that up? An' if you think Father Martello at Sacred Heart don't know what I do—even that I beat around the bush at confessions. Maybe a couple o' Hail Mary's he tells me is good enough for him an' gets him off the hook, but not for me any more. Looks like no way I'll be forgiven for the bad things I done; all those beatin's…never. I don't even know how God can let me off for that. But I want to keep askin' him, best way I know how. On my knees every day an' tryin' to live a good life. But if I do what Angelo's askin'…I may as well go to hell right now. "

No. Tony. No. You're too good for hell. God will forgive you. We'll think of something…what about the Lowensteins?"

"I can't talk to them, anymore. Look what I got 'em into already. I wish I didn't talk to them from the beginnin'. They're all-right guys an'…"

"It'd be okay. Talk to Joey. He's got a good head. He and his brothers, they all do. They like you. Maybe they'll come up with something. Talk to them, again. Please, Tony, it don't hurt to talk. We got nowhere else to go. And they got to figure out something for themselves, too. They're a part of this now whether they like it or not."

Patty? She was a seamstress, just out of Manhattan's

Needle Trades High School, working practically around the corner from the school in a garment center factory off 23rd Street where Tony showed up one day to do some official mob business with her boss. Seems the factory owner was making noise about the rising cost of the protection plan arrangement he had with The Boys and starting to say dumb things like communicating his concerns to the D.A.'s office.

So Tony, on his usual mission of righting a wrong as The Boys see the situation, gets out of the freight elevator and is walking through the noisy shop past the girls hunched over their Singers stitching up cheap flowery bathrobes and housecoats for the F.W. Woolworth Five & Ten trade. Patty gets out of her seat to pick up some more pieces—she's one of the many girls sewing on sleeves, and she and Tony bump into each other. Talk about fireworks and sparks and exploding stars and music; it was like something out of a book or a movie. If it wasn't love at first sight, it was the nearest thing. Even through Tony's flattened nose and scars Patty saw things beneath those physical imperfections, and while how he made his living was nowhere near obvious at that particular moment, she felt a tenderness and dignity that came through like headlights which lit up her heart.

It hit Tony, too; her long dark hair and sparkling eyes, and maybe Patty wasn't so movie star pretty, yet there was beauty coming from inside her Tony caught right away—a haymaker right between the eyes. He went down for the count!

He pulled himself together, remembered his mission, mumbled a "'scuse me," and went to the owner's office to make the proverbial offer the mark quickly learned that he couldn't refuse. Though, after meeting Patty, Tony's mind was far from 100% on the dirty deed at hand, he did come out of the office with a clear understanding that there was a clear understanding. Business first. Always business first!

Stopping at Patty's workstation on his return to the freight elevator, "You got a phone?" he asked. She eagerly passed the number to him and that was the beginning of a beautiful, but long courtship—Tony was never sure about bringing Patty into his kind of life, so he moved slowly. Very slowly.

"How come we only hold hands and you never kiss me?" Patty asked one night on the way to her place from a movie.

'You, you want me to kiss you?"

"I think about it."

"Me, too."

"So why not? Am I that ugly?"

"Ugly? You ain't ugly. You're the most beautiful girl I ever seen."

"Oh, Tony. So why not?"

"Didn't want you to think I was fresh or anythin'."

"Is a kiss going to hurt?"

"I don't think so. But it's—it's like a beginnin'."

"Of what?"

"Of more."

"Don't you have any more? Or want more?".

"I think so. Yeah, I got more. I want more. But there's things…."

"Things?"

"Yeah, things."

"Like what?"

"Like things I do. My work."

"You're a foreman on the docks, what's wrong with that."

"I do more."

"More of what?"

"You ain't gonna like what I do."

"How do I know until I know?"

"Cause it's hard for me to say."

"Just say it."

"I can't. I could lose you."

"Listen to me you big galoot, no matter what, you're not going to lose me. Unless you lie to your mother, beat up on kids, or steal money from the church box. Come on, tell me. What is it?"

"I don't lie to my mother 'cause I don't tell her much o' what I do. I don't steal. An' I don't beat up on kids."

So?"

"Like I said, I don't beat up on kids. I beat up on people."

"Excuse me?"

"Yeah, I beat up on people don't pay their dues, what they owe, don't follow the rules."

"Whose rules? What people?"

"The Boys. The family. Our rules. Makin' sure people s'posed to pay us, pay us…to protect 'em."

"Oh my God, so that's why you were at the factory when we met that first time. Oh my God. I never even thought…"

"I knew it. I'm gonna lose you."

"No, Tony. Wait. Wait a minute. Let me just get this straight. Are you what they call an 'enforcer'?"

"I think so. Yeah, that's what I am, an enforcer."

"And you actually beat up on people? You hit them. You hurt them? Tony, my love, don't tell me that's what you do."

"I knew it. I'm gonna lose you. shoulda never started this.…"

"No, Tony. No. You won't lose me. I love you. I really and truly love you. I wish…I wish you didn't do what you do, but I really love you and I know you're more than that. A lot more than that."

"I can't change, you know. It's bigger 'n you an' me. Really big."

"In time. In time, Tony. Maybe it'll change. Now I wish I didn't love you, but God forgive me, I do. I really, really do. 'Cause I know you're more than that. You're not like them. You can't be. I know it. And if you don't kiss me right now, hard, and take me home to bed, you will lose me and I'll never talk to you again."

When they finally did marry, there were always black clouds hanging over. The dark side of Tony's business that included the occasional late night work, and Patty's paranoia about his activities and involvement with The Boys that grew and festered. More recently, Tony's conscience pangs and feelings that God would forsake him, which would reflect on the adored son upon whom Tony doted. But there was always Patty's hope it could be changed. Always the hope.

6.

BETWEEN SHIP ARRIVALS THE LOWENSTEIN BROTHERS EACH have their other lives and interests, mostly focused on their families—with all their quirks and diversities.

Freddie's wife Fran, somewhat a control freak, demands things just right around the house, the upshot of her time as an abused child removed from her parents and farmed out to unhappy times in more foster homes than she can count or cares to remember. In spite of the propensity for mistreated children themselves becoming abusers, to the contrary, Fran loves and dotes on her two sons and has never done anything to harm them physically or mentally—except for her neatness craze that's inflicted on all the household members with no prejudices; beginning with labels in the fridge and pantry lined up like a grocery store display, shoes arranged just so, clothes in the closet—everything in its place, everything in perfect arrangement and order. Freddie takes relief from these annoying, but petty household pressures with his Casanova dalliances, holding his cool around the house, but letting out his frustrations with matinee quickies. He believes he keeps them secret. Fran, her senses extra keen due to her miserable childhood, knows otherwise. But she won't rock the boat, being comfortable with the generous income Freddie brings home, their attractive ranch-style home in an upscale neighborhood, and two good kids. In spite of Freddie's extra-curricular sexual antics and sometimes frustrations over her neurotic behavior, he maintains a deep love for Fran…and a strong bond with his two sons. A few times she'll make moderate threats to leave, but push comes to shove, she's always around the next morning. This life by comparison to her depressing upbringing is too good to sacrifice.

At every other opportunity, Freddie takes to fishing with sons Ben and Sam in Long Island Sound aboard The Gefilte Fish, the modest ten-year old 39-foot Chris Craft he and Joey and other volunteering family and friends put in a lot of hours patching-up and making seaworthy, and from which they all get a lot of pleasure fishing or just cruising and schmoozing. It's also great for entertaining the company's clients, and often even a few of The Boys, especially Eddie Lump Lump who takes to fishing with the same enthusiasm he takes to eating.

Ira and his wife Bea, with no kids, are true, self-indulging urbanites, taking in Broadway plays, the ballet, enjoying nights at the Metropolitan Opera, and testing and tasting an assortment of French and exotic cuisine at Manhattan restaurants of which there seems to be no end. College grad Bea, a lady of class, was the one who introduced Ira to the sophisticated life that he took to easily and gratefully. Never a snob, Bea entrances her audiences when she discusses music and theater. The divas and tenors, the arias, sets and librettos. The prima donnas, the dancers and the dances. The plays, the plots and the actors. Her eyes shine and her hands, arms and body become seductively dramatic as she shares her love of the arts. Ira adores her. With no kids, they completely enjoy their hedonistic lifestyle.

Joey? He's married to beautiful Shirley, the Lowenstein family baleboste (Jewish housewife and mother extraordinaire). Armed with hand-me-down recipes from her mother and aunts, every day Shirley turns her kitchen into an alluring, aroma-filled habitat. It's a wonder Joey isn't as huge as Eddie Lump Lump. The warmth and balance she puts into her cooking and baking is the same she doles out to those of the family coming to her with their troubles. It's a good and faithful marriage, and their daughters are as pretty and as active as Shirley. When not involved with work or doting on his girls, Joey tinkers with cars—doing tune-ups and minor repairs for his brothers, other relatives and friends. And taking photos with the German 35mm Leica he picked up from a dead Nazi SS officer during the Battle of the Bulge. There's a small, dark red spot on the back of the camera that won't come out no matter how hard Joey tries…and he has never spoken about how the German soldier had died.

This day? The brothers were in the office feasting on bursting-at-the-seams pastrami-on-rye sandwiches, new dill pickles, cream sodas and celery tonics Ira'd brought over from Katz's Deli on Houston Street in the lower east side of Manhattan. Katz's is a treasured institution New Yorkers of all backgrounds have nominated to the delicatessen hall of fame—famous for its WWII slogan, "Send a salami to your boy in the army."

You don't have to be Jewish to enjoy Katz's tantalizing and stomach-stuffing array of oversized smoked meat sandwiches, chopped chicken liver platters, knishes, kasha and kishka, salami and eggs, chicken soup, selected from a menu that goes on and on…and on. Those with huge appetites who can still find the room will finish off with a New York style cheesecake…the entire meal washed down with seltzer, the carbonated water known as the Jewish national beverage.

"You always liked pastrami better'n corned beef, didn't you," asked Joey.

"I like it's smokier, maybe even spicier, and the crusty trim on the outside," said Ira, holding his sandwich up for all to see. "But I wouldn't turn down a good kosher corned beef sandwich, either."

"Hey," asked Joey, "Did you eat your banana today? You gotta listen to Chiquita Banana. You know…a banana a day…."

"Of course," answered Ira, "helps my blood pressure."

"Constipation, too."

"Thanks for that. You sure know how to ruin a guy's appetite."

"You know that bananas are good for mosquito bites?"

"Yeah, I read all the promo material from United Fruit; good for brain power, depression, hangovers, heartburn, morning sickness, nerves, PMS—a good reason for your wife to eat one every morning, not to mention stress, strokes, ulcers and warts. It's a goddamn cure-all elixir. Imagine, and it all starts with some muchacho in a straw hat swinging a machete."

"And never put bananas," Joey sang the final words of the famous Chiquita banana radio commercial—somewhat off key, "in the refrig-erator. Oh no, no, no."

It's another miserably cold New York rainy day. The docks are clear—no ships, no trucks, no longshoremen, nobody hustling bananas or other cargo down the gangways into the waiting trucks. No bustle. The icy rains driving down heavy from a gray sky, washing away the dock debris from the day before. The wind churning up the Hudson River where boat traffic is down, and a persistent, penetrating deep foghorn cutting through the pelting downpour playing a mournful duet with the lonesome buoy bells, creating a waterfront symphony that few people hear. Those who do, know this is the mysterious and enchanting New York Harbor through which all kinds of living and other things come and go.

A good day to be at the Terminal and to be sitting comfy in JIF's office with the electric heater turned up high. A weekly business ritual during which the brothers checklist ship arrivals, break down customer orders, schedule the gypsy truckers, and discuss business in general. Rosie, normally in attendance on these prep' days, has the day off—from the office that is; a JIF customer is in from Detroit and Rosie's showing him the town, among other things.

"Gunnar Ericson's wife called? Him and his truck won't be on call for a week."

"He picked up a long haul?"

"Nah, that shmagegga—you know how he likes to show off opening beer bottles with his teeth?"

"Don't tell me he broke one."

"Not one, three. And cut his mouth real bad. Got stitches and can't eat."

"These guys work around here? They're all meshuginah. Crazy like loons."

"Including us, I think."

"You hear about the snake the Mad Russian pulled out of a stem the other day?" asked Joey. "Big like a hawser, they say."

"Yeah, heard he whipped it around like a bull whip, like Zorro, smacking its head against a dock cleat. I think the Russian's brain got frozen in Siberia."

"They say it was a poisonous one."

"Most of them are from down there. Wonder how they survive the trip."

"Feeding on the spiders, I guess."

"Seen a lot of those, too. Big hairy ones. A miracle the stevies don't get stung."

"Spiders don't sting. They bite."

"Bite. Sting. What's the difference? Both could kill you."

"Looks like the Rossi Brothers in Cleveland are up for a full load next week."

"Reminds me. One of us gotta go to a wedding there; Vito Rossi's oldest daughter. Fran and me are tied up that weekend with the boys' football game. It's a big regional."

"I'll go," said Joey. Vito and me—we get along pretty good. And his wife and my Shirley seemed to hit if off last time. Freddie, maybe you can take the kids for the weekend."

"No problem. Lots of excitement at the game, lots of other kids around, they'll have a good time. Just lemme check with Fran—see if we can fit into her schedule. You know Fran!"

"Good," said Ira. "I was going to beg off anyway. There's a ballet that weekend; Bea's got us upfront seats."

"Anybody want my other half of this sandwich? I'm full already. I can't eat the whole thing." Joey said.

"Naaah, put it in the fridge. Somebody'll finish it to-morrow. Got enough trouble eating mine."

"Wonder we don't die from that famous Jewish dis-ease—heartburn."

"Don't talk about dying…we ain't done with the Tony issue and I got a feeling neither are The Boys."

"Heard anything more?"

"No." said Joey. Tony's been kind of quiet. Called in

and said he wasn't coming today, which is okay, since there's nothing for him."

"Wonder what they'll do."

"You never know. They could chase him."

"Is that like they throw him out and he can't associate with none of the made guys any more?"

"It's a possibility."

"I don't think so. That's too easy. Angelo keeps his family tight. He won't let anybody go he ain't sure of."

"Why can't he be sure of Tony? Always done what they asked, never said nothin' to nobody I know of. A real square guy—the side we've been involved with, anyway."

"Maybe if Tony said he just wanted out 'cause he was tired or sick or something. Or, Patty putting the pressure on him. But to say he got religion, I think that scares The Boys. People get fanatic about religion—you never know. A lot of conscience comes into play and next thing you know the sinner's confessing anything and everything to anybody'd listen."

"Whyn't they ice him? Make it simple for everybody."

"Come on, Freddie, you don't mean that," said Joey.

"I guess not, but why not? Why don't they just put him away?"

"Because they have a bizarre sense of family...of loyalty," said Ira. "Besides, they like the idea of control, holding on to something long as they can control it. Gives 'em that sense of power."

"I wish they'd give him a pass. He could really help us out a lot of ways."

"Frankly, I wish he didn't get us involved. I don't like us being involved any more than we are," said Ira.

"How the hell can you beat up people for a living? Especially a family man like Tony?"

"Split personality," said Ira. "To begin with, on the surface, best we know, Tony's not a complex person. Probably looks at life in a similar simple way; one half of him has no social values; he hits people because it's his job and he doesn't even think about it as hurting. It's salesmanship—with a bat. It's what he does for a living. The only thing he thinks about is the end result, not what it's doing to the guy, or the guy's family. The other half of his personality is more like normal—whatever normal is these days; with feelings for his wife and kid and his friends and even The Boys. And maybe some sense of social responsibilities, and somehow he's able to keep the two apart."

"Some amateur psychologist you are," mocked Freddie.

"Momma always wanted a doctor in the family," said Joey.

"It's as good an explanation you're going to get from some high-priced Park Avenue shrink," Ira tossed back, "who's never even been down to the docks, except maybe for a vacation cruise, or to Little Italy and Arthur Avenue for pizza and a bowl of spaghetti. What do they know goes on in the real world? We're the ones in the real world. We're the ones dealing with the bad guys every day. We're the ones fighting to make a living. Compromising our own values day after day. I don't know how you guys explain some of what we have to do—who we do business with, to your kids. I'm kinda glad Bea and I don't have any. Wouldn't know what to say to them."

"You got a point," said Joey. "But we picked this business—the good with the bad, and until we close down or sell our customer list to another freight company… or a goody-goody hotshot D.A. and the Feds get a major probe going and busts the mob…or better yet they bump each other off—of which we read in the papers every other week, but not often enough, we got to dance with the girls we invited. They won't let us do it any other way anyway."

"Just a few more years," said Ira. "Just a few more years and our investments'll pay off big, and Freddie can spend the rest of his life on The Gefilte Fish—even a bigger one... Joey, you can move to Florida like you've always dreamed and take all the pictures of palm trees and slender blonde shicksas and zaftig Jewish chicks in teeny bikinis all you want...and Bea and I can enjoy box seats at every opera house around the world. For now, and in the foreseeable future, there's gold in these bananas, brothers, so let the economy stay solid, let's keep our customers happy, stay on good terms with The Boys, and all we need is just a few more good years."

"From your lips to the banana god's ears."

The next morning: "You guys have always been good to me," said Rosie, "never asked about my other life, treat me square...couldn't ask for no better bosses. But I got to talk to you about Tony...and something else."

"He done something?" asked Freddie.

"No, he's a sweetheart...I mean we gotta talk about his problem with The Boys."

"What do you have to do with it? Somebody say something?"

"I don't know how to say this, I guess I'll just have to come out with it."

"Can't be that bad, Rosie."

"It's not nice and you guys deserve better."

"Okay, already...what is it?"

"Nobody's going to hit me, right?"

"Come on Rosie, what do you think we are? Like them? What's going on?"

"I don't think I like this."

"No. You're not going to like it. But I got to get it out. Okay. Here goes. I'm a plant. The Boys put me in here to keep tabs on you. Keep them informed."

"Informed of what?"

"Anything gives them an edge. They got somebody on the inside with most every major player they do business and they put me in here."

"Jesus Christ, Rosie; how could you? After all we do for you."

"You're kidding, aren't you? You got to be putting us on!"

"Wish I was. 'Cause what I'm telling you could get me killed. It's not something I wanted to do. "

"So why the hell did you do it?"

"Not much choice. You all know my baby brother's in the State pen doing his time for that felony. But Angelo said they'd get him out sooner and also make sure he wouldn't get hurt long as he was in. You know what can happen in those places. Especially my brother, who's kind of a fragile kid. Honest, it's not something I wanted to do, but they got their ways."

"Rosie, Rosie, we trusted you. And I thought you and me had something going." Freddie moaned.

"We did Freddie. We did. First time I saw you in Baltimore, even if it was a setup. And we still do, in a way. You're special. You really are. You're all special. The rest of it? With them? A job. Just a job. Not to mention I like sex, as you know. As for this, I'm really sorry. I never told them anything important. Really. You guys are clean and there was really never anything to tell them. You guys are like babes in the woods."

"You tellin' us."

"So why all this now? Especially if what you say about it could get you killed is true?"

"Two reasons. First, through the grapevine, and I'm even not supposed to know this, word leaked out that my brother got raped and beaten up bad by a couple of screwed-up inmates. Almost killed him. He's in the prison hospital in ICU. So far The Boys don't know I know and I got to keep it that way. So much for Angelo and his thugs protecting the poor kid. As for getting him out early, I don't think that was ever a plan. Keeping me on the hook all the time, that was their lousy plan. And second, 'cause you guys are in real danger what with this Tony thing."

"How's that?"

"Worst you ever did Joey, was pick up that German camera and take up photography."

"It's a harmless hobby."

"Not if you're the one taking the pictures of Tony doing a big hit."

"What big hit? What pictures? What do you mean big hit?"

"I guess Tony didn't tell you…"

"Tell us what?"

"They said they'd let him out only if he does a big one. Which means killing somebody. They want pictures of him doing it…and they want Joey here, taking the pictures."

"While Tony's killing some poor schlub they want me taking pictures? What are they, crazy? They gotta be meshuga."

"Never said they weren't. It's their way of covering all the bases. This way they got the goods on Tony to keep his mouth shut what with all he's seen, done and knows, and they got the goods on Joey and you guys if—whatever. It's like insurance. Killing two birds with one stone, pardon the expression."

"Makes sense for them, doesn't it? They'll have something over our heads and start pushing us to haul their illegal crap our stateside routes and to Canada."

"I'll be damned. The dirty wop bastards. Friends, huh? Friends as long as we pay our monthlies, huh? As long as we bring nice presents to their weddings and confirmations. As long as... I'll be damned."

"Thing is," Rosie said, "Tony hasn't signed off on it, yet. "

"Does he have a choice?"

"A couple of years, you said, Ira?" grumbled Freddie. A couple of years and we're on permanent holiday? It's gonna be permanent, all right. Permanently dead, or at the very least permanently under their thumb, what with evidence like that. I'll tell you what, like if we ever had a contract these guys just broke it. I figure we don't owe them a thing anymore and I might even take Dominic for a walk down the pier and beat the crap out of him."

"You do that and the cops'll find what's left of us stuffed in a garbage bin somewhere in a pile of our own rotting banana peels. Or, as Dominic likes to say, at the bottom of the river.' Not a good idea, Freddie. Not a good idea."

"You got a better one?"

"No. I have no idea how we get out of this. No idea."

"What," asked Joey, "if I refuse to take the pictures? That was a stupid question, wasn't it?"

"Yeah, if you want to find your wife and kids without a husband and father. Maybe even you without a wife and kids. They're not above that, you know. How the hell do you say no to these crazies? They kill their own, for god sakes. You don't say no if you want to live."

"I think we got major tsoris."

7.

"WHERE'S JOEY?" DAPPER DOMINIC ASKED AS HE ENTERED JIF's office. "I gotta see Joey."

"On his way to Schenectady," answered Rosie. "One of the gypsies broke down and he's following a replacement rig so they can switch the load before the fruit freezes and still make the delivery to Mastrioanni's in Buffalo."

"I'll never know how he can leave you in the office all alone, Rosie. I would never let you out of my sight. Not with a built like you got. If you know what I mean."

"What a sweet talker you are, Dominic. How come you only talk?"

"Ahh, it's the Italian way. All talk, no action. You know what I mean? Besides, if I fooled around, Marie'd cut off my you-know-whats. You do not know Marie. She'd do it, too. And then what kind of Italian stud would I be without my you-know-whats? Don't answer that. Anybody else around?"

"Freddie just went to the john. Be back any minute—oh, here he is. Look who's here, Freddie."

Freddie entered the room, stopped when he saw Dominic, wondering what the thug was doing here. It wasn't the end of the month.

Dominic answered the unasked question; "We gotta talk, Freddie. Let's take a walk down the pier."

The ritual persists; the long walk, the guarded looks left, right, front, back, the half-whispers.

At the end of the pier, "So what's up, Dominic? Any problems?"

"Naaah, not yet, anyways. Just want to make sure all the i's are crossed the t's dotted, so to speak. You know what I mean?"

"I don't know what you mean. We made our monthly. What else is there?"

"Ahh, Freddie, don't play dumb with me. This Tony thing—it's got the boss a little tense. And me, too. And that's not a good thing. We are only askin' for Tony do a major hit and Joey take some pictures like he is good at, and we ain't sure what Tony's got in mind."

"What pictures? Pictures of what? What hit? What the hell are you talking about?" Freddie couldn't let on without jeopardizing Rosie.

"Tony didn't say nothin'?"

"About what?"

"About if he wants out and if you guys want to take him on, he's got to do a whack job and Joey proves he done it with the pictures. You didn't know?"

"You're kidding."

"We don't kid about things like this. Just lookin' to protect ourselves, if you know what I mean."

"Holy shit, Dominic. We're just banana truckers. You're asking something we don't do every day. Hell, we don't do at all, 'cept the goddamn war. Maybe something you goombahs do day-to-day, but not the Lowenstein brothers."

"Don't shit in your pants, Freddie. All we want is pictures; none of you Lowensteins do a major hurt on nobody. That's what Tony's for. It's his job."

"And what a lousy job—pressuring a guy to ice somebody, especially a good dude like Tony. Then dragging us in on it?"

"Good dude? Tony? Good dude? Hey, you ain't never seen that goomba in action; breakin' arms and knees like they was toothpicks. And what he does with that Louisville? He'd bat an easy .500 was he in the Yankee lineup. Tony ain't all the sweetheart you think he is, if you know what I mean."

"All we know is he wants out. He wants to face his God like a mensch, not a goon."

"You calling us goons?"

"You got another name for it?"

"I ain't used to this wise guy talk, especially from you, Freddie. You've always been cooperative. Never with the insults. Why the change?"

"You guys don't give me much choice, asking us to be a part of a murder."

"Shhhh, Freddie. Shhhh. Even these piers has ears. I guess I better try this another way. As we all know, the talk around is Avery Freight is in line to buy JIF when things are right, with a juicy couple of years management contract, and it'd be a nice retirement for you and your brothers. So a little cooperation with this business we got at hand would only mean that there would be no monkey wrench in the works, so to speak. Know what I mean? Besides, Avery's a big national operation. We ain't so sure they'd be as cooperative, as friendly as you guys, so we'd have to think it over about whether you sellin' out to them is to our benefit or not. Know what I mean? Do you know what I fuckin' mean?"

"You wouldn't screw that up."

"Wouldn't want to, but you never know. You force our hand…."

"I ought break your head," fumed Freddie.

As quick as a cobra strike, Dominic had a switchblade to Freddie's throat; "You ain't fighting the fuckin' Japs or the Chinks, Freddie. I know you was a war hero. And you did your share. But this is me, Dominic. A hundred guys like me from the streets coulda won the fuckin' war in two weeks. Nobody, especially you, is breakin' my head. You damned kikes, you ain't supposed to be fighters."

"You don't call me a kike!"

"Don't be so touchy. We know you call us dagos and grease balls and wops and guineas when we ain't around. You know what? I'll tell you what! I don't give a fuck what you call me. You make your monthlies…you talk Tony into doing the hit…and you get Joey to take those god-damn pictures. You do what we want when we want it and how we want it and things'll stay cool. Know what I mean? Do-you-know-what-I-fucking-mean?"

Dominic withdrew the knife and stepped back, at which point Freddie, combat veteran of two wars with a grisly history of enemy blood on his hands, in just a flash sensed an edge, his entire body giving in to his old bat-tlefield instincts; a smell of fear instantaneously turning to a self-preservation mode he thought had been pushed back into the recesses of his mind. That all-senses alarm-ing stench suddenly filling his nostrils and boiling his blood. Automatically he raked his elbow across Domi-nic's head, following up with a smash to the surprised goombah's face with a powerful left cross that reeled the thug back into a mooring post and then flying off the edge of the pier, arms and legs flailing, into the icy Hud-son River.

Down Dominic went into the dark freezing water, coming up once slapping at the water and screaming,

"You stupid fuckin' kike. I can't swim. Throw me some-thin', you sonofabitch. Throw me a rope or somethin'."

Freddie thought, as he did when he was a warrior, "It's him or me. Better him." Or maybe it was not even thinking at all. Looking down at Dapper Dominic with his $500 cashmere coat sucking up the black water like a sponge and seeing the number two gangster struggling to stay afloat, Freddie yelled down, "Drown you bastard goniff, drown and die and get out of our lives."

While the strong Hudson River current moved him further from the pier, Dapper Dominic was not aware that the lower Hudson is actually a tidal estuary, with tidal in-fluence extending as far as the Federal Dam at Troy, and that strong tides make parts of New York Harbor difficult and dangerous to navigate…or swim. During the winter, ice floes drift south or north, depending upon the tides, with the fresh water discharge at the river's mouth in New York approximately 21,400 cubic feet (606 cubic meters) per second.

None of this was on his mind as his waterlogged cash-mere coat, custom-made by Rizzo the Tailor on Arthur Avenue up in the Bronx, dragged him down. While the beautiful Hudson River—sometimes called America's Rhine, stunned his muscles and mind with hypothermia, filled his lungs, and drowned him. The strong tides mov-ing the body further downriver toward Staten Island and points east.

Still shaking, Freddie returned to the office more con-cerned about his brothers' wrath than any revenge from The Boys—if they ever found out what happened. Important business decisions and actions, he recalled the three brothers agreeing—almost in blood, are made by all three together. No exceptions. And knocking the number two mob henchman into the river is about as important a business action, or mis-action, as ever would be made. Lucky, he thought, Joey's on a mercy errand saving a load, and right now he'd only have to deal with Ira—which can be bad enough considering Ira's ultra-conservative streak on any business or social decisions. Screwing up a shipment's paperwork is enough to get Ira going. Killing one of The Boys? Don't even ask!

Freddie sighed with relief. Ira wasn't in. Rosie was.

"You tell nobody," Freddie warned Rosie, "that Dominic was anywhere near this place today."

"Why? What's wrong?"

"You don't want to know. Just remember, Dominic nowhere near here today."

"Look," snapped Rosie. "I'm in all of this just as deep as you guys. So you better tell me what's going on. Besides, I know The Boys a lot better than you, so maybe I can help if it's that serious."

"It's that serious."

"Like what?"

"I just killed Dominic."

"You what???"

"The stupid shmuck pulled a knife on me so I slugged him and he tripped and fell in the Hudson. He's probably going through The Narrows right now."

"Oh my god, Freddie. Are you okay?"

"Yeah. A little shaky. Ain't done anything like this since…" and he cut it short. "I'll be okay. The sonovabitch called me a kike and even threatened to screw up our deal with Avery. That stupid sonovabitch. Talking about Tony icing somebody and Joey there with his camera, like you said. He'd even have done in Joey if Joey refused to take the pictures. That sonovabitch. Had a goddamn knife to my throat. A steel blade this big. Sonovabitch!"

"You sure he's gone. Didn't swim away?"

"He was no swimmer. The current's too fast and the water's too cold. He was a goner in minutes. Maybe seconds."

"Oh my God. His car. Dominic's car. His Caddy. He parks it right out front. We have to get rid of it."

"I did. Somehow I remembered. Broke the window, hot wired, and pushed it into the river. Maybe it'll meet Dominic out in the Atlantic. Shit. My heart's still goin' a mile a minute."

Okay. Okay. Calm down. Let's get you a drink. You could use a one. And I need some thinking time."

As she poured a neat Famous Grouse for Freddie, she said, "You know Freddie, the fewer people know about this the better."

"What do you mean?"

"I mean I wouldn't even tell your brothers. That way if it comes to them being asked they come off real honest when they say they don't know anything. Nobody'd think they were involved."

"I gotta tell my brothers."

"I wouldn't do it, Freddie. Better leave them out of it for now. Nobody saw you at the end of the pier, did they?"

"No one. I checked around good. Deader than a doornail out there."

"Let's keep this between you and me till a better time. Just you and me. Please. I'm telling you, Freddie, it's the best way. You did not see Dominic today. He never talked to you about what they want Tony and Joey to do. You're stupid about the whole thing. Okay?"

"Okay. For now, anyway."

I mean it, Freddie. Nothing to nobody. We'll see how it all plays out. You know I still feel something for you…

even though I was put up to everything. You're a great guy and because of all that went on with us—and a little fooling around now and then since, we know we can keep a secret, right? Except I still don't know how Fran found out you were sleeping around. You don't talk in your sleep, do you?"

"No. I don't talk in my sleep. And I'm not sure I'm gonna get much sleep after today."

"Remember, Dominic threatened you. You had to protect yourself. Times like that accidents happen. That's it. Accidents happen. Let me pour you another one. It's gonna be a long day."

8.

"I WAS WONDERING," SAID EDDIE LUMP LUMP, WHOSE bountiful body well-corroborates his nickname, to Gino the Grip, on their way to JIF's office to see what they could see about the missing Dominic, "all this time you never say what you did in the Army."

"Nothin' to talk about. Wasn't much. Big waste o' time. I bought me a 4F card, but they got me anyways an' sent me to Fort Dix, over in Jersey. What a dump hole. A hunnert losers inna crummy barracks snorin', fartin', some even bawlin' like babies. Bunch of mamalukes. They got this ougats—a nuthin' Polack Sergeant from Philly with big balls tellin' ya when to hit the sack, when to get up, when to go to chow—real dog food I wouldn't even feed a dog, I tell ya. An' he's in my face alla time. 'Hey you, guinea,' he calls me, 'stan' up straight, fix your hat, shine yer shoes,' a real boombots. I tell him, baffangul, get outta my face; stop all this stugats (bullshit). Just gimme a gun and send me over to kill some Japs and Germans and leave me alone. He grabs me an' shoves his schnozzola against my face so I knee the stunad—the stupido moron, in the gonads, and he doubles up. One uppercut an' a chop to the back of his thick Polack head an' he's on the ground an' I'm puttin' my shiny new GI boots to his friggin' ribs. Next thing ya know I'm in the stockade for the duration.

But it wasn't bad. A couple of the screws turns out to be they was paisanos—from Boston an' Detroit; I grease 'em with a fin each week and I get easy duty peelin' a few potatoes and sweepin' floors 'til I'm out with a DD and I'm home with you and The Boys and everythin's back to what I like. That was it. No John Wayne crap. No nothin'. Wasn't so bad for you, what I hear."

"No. Business as usual, but we had some fun. You know, runnin' numbers and things for Fat Frankie, some black market stuff with ration stamps, nylons, whiskey, gas coupons, T-bones, things like that. Also, Frankie had a string of hookers working downtown so we got a little puttana the off times. Oh yeah, we'd go down to Times Square and roll the drunks, mostly soldiers and sailors. Always good for a few bucks and a few laughs. Tell you one thing, we stayed away from them hard-assed Marines. They'd go back and bring a whole friggin' army of 'em lookin' for us. Fuckin' killers."

"Too bad I missed it. A lot better'n I had. Ya know what I missed most? All the Italian food I grew up. Ganol', capicol', manigott', ricotta…used to lay in the sack dreamin' about a table full of it."

"You makin' me hungry."

"You? You're always hungry. Why doncha open a restaurant?"

"Ya know what? That ain't so funny. Been somethin' I been thinkin' about."

"No kiddin'! Where would you open up?"

"Little Italy. Maybe even up in the Bronx on Arthur Avenue. Near where people come for good Italian cookin'. Ya know it's all in the sauce, like my Nonna made. Italian restaurant ya make a good tomato sauce an' everythin' else comes together. She even made the tomato paste from scratch…an' even her own bread crumbs. She taught Momma an' the sisters, and I learned by watchin' hangin' around the kitchen."

"You'd do Sicilian style?"

"I dunno. Checkin' it out there's a lot of choice; ya got the mangiapolenta style—for the polenta eaters from north Italy, mangiafagioli—the bean eaters from the middle o' the boot, an' mangiamaccheroni—the macaroni eaters from the south. Olive oil for the south, butter for the north. Lotsa picks. Maybe I'd do a mixed menu brings in everybody. I even gotta name."

"Yeah? Ain't gonna be Lump Lump's, is it?"

"Very funny. Naah. I'm gonna call it Nonna's Italian Bistro."

"I like that. You really been thinkin' about this."

"Yeah, somethin' I'd really like to do. But it's on hold till this Tony thing blows over. Gettin' out don't seem to be easy. Although I'd just be running a eatin' joint an' still able to help out when there's a call. Wouldn't want to lose touch with my block buddies."

"Yeah. Enough goin' on right now to give ya agita, a heartburn we don't need on top of everythin' else."

When the pair lumbered into JIF's office, with Eddie an avid angler anxious to see Freddie and talk about some springtime fishing in Long Island Sound on board The Gefilte Fish, only Rosie was around. Eddie had often been a guest on Freddie's boat, trolling and casting for striped bass, fluke, flounder, or whatever comes in for the chum and takes the hook bait. Freddie has to double—even triple—up on the sandwiches and beer when Eddie's on board; but it's keeping good relations with The Boys, and Eddie is an okay fishing companion. Fishing or eating, he's one happy goombah.

"Hey Rosie," said Gino, "when's my turn on that beautiful body of yours?"

"A classy guy like you, Gino—you don't want sloppy seconds, especially after I do your boss."

"Always kidding, huh Rosie. Always kidding. You, you really doing Angelo?"

"That's only between Angelo and me, Gino. And I wouldn't go asking him, if I were you. Wouldn't be a smart move now, would it? Right Eddie?"

"Not somethin' I would do. Nope. My Momma didn't raise no stupido."

"So what brings you handsome guys here?"

"She's not such a dumb chick, Eddie, is she? A lot more there than just a body. Okay. Let's get to business. Dominic, you see 'im? Last we heard he was coming here to talk with the Jew-boys. Day before yesterday. He show up?"

"Nope. I was in the office all day, and no Dominic."

"Funny. He said he was comin'." Eddie said.

"Who else was here?" Gino asked.

"Day before yesterday? Let me think. Uh, Joey was on the road. Ira was out, and Freddie was here, just for a short bit, and left early so on his way home he could stop at the stationary store and pick up some typewriter ribbons and stuff we need for the office. There a problem?"

"Eddie and me here, and the rest, we're hopin' there's no problem. Just we ain't heard from Dominic and it ain't like him to be outta touch. We're checkin' everywhere."

"Gee, I'm sorry Gino. Wish I could help you. But no Dominic around here maybe a week."

"Sure?"

"Of course I'm sure."

"If you hear somethin' Rosie, you call us. You got the

number." He turns to leave, then turns back. "You and Angelo, huh?"

They left, Gino blowing Rosie a kiss, Eddie waving goodbye, saying, "Tell Freddie I'm on for his first spring fishin' trip."

Rosie finally let out her breath that she was holding in for it seemed like forever.

The last stem of the day was hung inside the truck, the final blanket draped, and Joey was doing his usual and thorough last-minute check while Tony adjusted the temperature dials on the heater. "Okay, Tony?"

"Working good, Joey. Better tell Sy when he's on the road to make sure he goes over the propane tank settin's every hour. Gonna be a cold night for the fruit. I'm finished here; goin' up to the office."

"Sy," Joey yelled to the driver, "She's all yours. Keep checking the temps and the tanks and don't let these green babies freeze. Call when you get to Akron. You got my home number. Drive careful and don't get stopped for speeding!"

Damn, it was cold out on the pier. Freezing winds were coming in off the river bearing a few snowflakes and Joey was always worried about the trucks hitting ice or blinding snowstorms on the New York Thruway and Jersey, Pennsylvania and Ohio Turnpikes, that could be the cause of a layover or even an accident. In good weather these multi-lane highways were a dispatcher's best friends with trucks getting to their destinations on and even before schedule. When winter weather turns especially sour, these northeastern highways are dangerous and unpredictable roads to disaster. All over the place, multi-vehicle pile-ups, jackknifed semis, skidding and out of control passenger cars and pickups, black ice, whiteouts; always something for Joey to worry about. Including the Rest Stop hookers who, if they were legit prostitutes only took care of a trucker's away-from-home needs. If they weren't, they'd not only take care of his sexual needs, they'd take leave with his wallet, which not only led to late deliveries, but also spoiled fruit with the driver distracted enough to forgot to check the temperature. Always something to worry about.

Joey raced back inside the terminal and up to the office, anxious to get someplace warm. Rosie was at the typewriter, Ira was on the phone, Freddie was pouring a scotch, and Tony was sitting on the edge of the cracked leather divan rubbing his hands warm; he'd been looking forward to the end of the day to talk to the brothers.

"Hey, a little early for that stuff, isn't it?" Joey asked Freddie, as he moved his frozen hands over the portable heater.

"Just trying to take the chill off." Freddie so desperately wanted to tell his brothers about Dominic, but he sensed Rosie might be right. The less they know, the better—the safer they would be. The whisky would do double duty; warm him up and maybe also tranquilize his nerves, shaky at best since the Dominic incident. When he returned from Korea he'd thought—he'd hoped, his killing days were history. The camaraderie in the Corps was great. He'd always liked the solidarity and the comradeship, even as a Jew among a company of redneck jarheads. But he never liked the killing, even the Japs or the Commies. He did it because it was them or him, and did it well. But never took to liking it like some of the others even taking gold teeth and ears as souvenirs. Not Freddie; just wasn't in his makeup. He shivered some more, remembering.

"It's cold as a gunnery sergeant's heart out there," he said to Joey. "Want a shot?"

"Sure, if it'll warm me up."

"There's some hot water in the thermos, Tony. " Rosie said. "Make yourself a cup of tea. Good you stay away from the booze like these 'shickas.'"

"'You pick up Yiddish pretty good for a shicksa. Shicka, shicksa, funny how those two words are so similar," teased Ira. "And you don't drink at all, right Rosie?"

"Nary a drop of liquor will ever cross my rosy red lips," she responded. "Except for a small glass of Dom Perignon on New Year's Eve. A girl's got to keep her wits about her at all times."

"Dom Perignon. Me oh my. Always the classy lady," Joey said. Turning to Tony, "What's up, Tony? First time you been around in a couple of days. Lots on your mind, eh?"

"You betcha," Tony agreed. "Lots."

"Well," sighed Ira, "Let's get everything out in the open and see what we can see. Lock the door, will you Rosie? We don't need unexpected company. Oh yeah, one question Rosie, now that you can talk, is this place bugged?"

"No. They were just relying on me. No bugs here. They got them other places, but not here."

"I guess we're not important enough," laughed Joey.

"What do you mean not important enough," asked Rosie. "Didn't they put me here?"

"Just for the eye candy," Freddie volunteered, a little more relaxed after a couple of shots of the mellowing scotch.

"Hah, hah!"

"Okay, let's get serious," said Ira. "Tony's got an issue and that gives us an issue. Whether we like it or not, The

Boys have got us all tied together like The Marx Brothers. Whatever solution we come up for him is a solution for us, and vice versa. So anybody got any ideas? Don't hold back; even something ridiculous might spark something we can use."

"I ain't the brightest guy in the world," said Tony, "but one thing I see is The Boys, once they got their minds set on somethin', they're like bulldogs. They don't let go. They want me to ice somebody…they want Joey to take pictures when I do…an' whatever we say ain't gonna change nothin'. They always get what they want."

"Then we gotta come up with something they think satisfies 'em, but still don't do what they want?" said Ira.

"What are you, some kind of miracle worker? The Boys ain't stupid, you know."

"No, not stupid, but maybe if we're smart enough, maybe we can fool 'em. Don't you think three New York Jews aren't smarter than those brainless street hoods who think through their greaseball tucheses? No offense, Tony. We'll fool them, alright. One way or another."

"Like how?"

"Don't laugh, but I'm thinking about illusions. Trick photography."

"For chrissakes Ira, you know I'm not that good in the darkroom."

"Not in the darkroom, you schlimazel. We fake the killing. We're not talking about moving pictures with sound here," said Ira. "Though I'll never know why they never thought of it—maybe it really don't matter to them. They just want the intimidation, getting and keeping us scared. Involved. Believing we believe they got the goods on us. Make us do things. Anyway, these are, whatchamacallit, still shots, right? That Nazi-shmatzy camera of yours? A

35mm? It takes one shot at a time, right? So we stage each picture one at a time."

"You mean I don't smack him on the head with the bat?" Tony asked, hopefully.

"That's right. It only looks like. We use ketchup. We tie cement blocks—but with slipknots. We toss him over so Joey can get some pictures, then we fish him out—fast! We go for the Academy Award."

"So what's Sammy the Spic doing all this time?"

"He's going along with it all. Don't you see? He don't want to die, so we fake the whole schlimazel and Sammy disappears…we get a signed statement from Sammy it's all staged that we show to the cops or anybody thinks we actually did it should The Boys ever bring it up for whatever reason which I would doubt they ever would anyway. But with these goombahs, you can't predict. So we prepare for the worst scenario. When it's done, Sammy packs his toothbrush and his one silk shirt and very quietly and very quickly goes back to Cuba or wherever the hell he came from, which I think he's happy as shit to do considering the alternative, and we go on with our business until we're ready to get out, maybe sooner if we can, to get away from all this mishegah. That simple. What do you think Tony? It's your call."

"I don't know."

"Me neither," said Joey. "We're not actors, you know. Could end up looking phony."

"I think I got that covered." Ira said with confidence. "You know those soap opera TV shows they do over at NBC in Rockefeller Center? My neighbor, a fagele, but one of the good guys, is an assistant director who works on those shows and maybe he'd give us some theatrical pointers."

"I don't think it's a good idea getting somebody else involved?"

"It'd be okay. I'll present it to him like an idea—hypothetically. Like a pitch for a new TV show. Or like maybe just asking out of curiosity how they fake those kindsa things. The Boys don't even know he exists, so there's no way to tie him into us."

"What if The Boys want to be there when we're doin' it?

"We make sure they're not. We find a way."

"This is crazy!"

"I know it is. You got a better idea?"

"This ain't a Broadway play, you know. Or a cocka-mamie TV show. This is for real. We could get ourselves killed."

"You could get hit by a Manhattan Transit bus or a Yellow Cab crossing 42nd Street, too," said Ira. "I don't know if we have much choice. How about we should hold a vote?"

One thing you can count on with the Lowenstein boys is that they're street smart. Growing up in Harlem, in the twenties and thirties, before southern black families began replacing the Jews who had begun moving up the economic ladder and migrating to the Upper West Side, it was a time when Harlem had the third largest Jewish population in the world, it was still the hostile and harsh streets of New York and all that went with them. To survive, you had to live by your wits—or how fast you could run. Especially if you were a Jew living in a mixed neighborhood and zigzagging to and from the Old Broadway Synagogue on 125th Street, or the library, through mocking, and sometimes physical gauntlets of taunting Irish, German or Italian kids. Or even battling bullies of your own kind on your own block; seems there was always a street heavy, or two or three or more, in every ethnic community. Didn't matter Jewish, Irish, Italian, Black; always a schoolyard or neighborhood bully. So you learned how to survive, one way or another. Then there were the city schoolyards and playgrounds where, to keep playing softball, handball and basketball, only the winners stayed on for the next game. Losers sat sipping sodas, tossing pennies, flipping baseball cards, waiting another turn. So you became more competitive, smarter, sharper. That's the way you stayed on the field. And now, now the Lowenstein's street smarts were being put to a different kind of test—one that could cost them their business…or even their lives.

9.

ANGELO WAS CONCERNED. BAD ENOUGH HE HASN'T HEARD from Dominic, but even Dominic's wife is in the dark, and so his mother. This is not like his number two guy, reliable to a fault. You tell Dominic to do something he's fucking Johnny-on-the-spot. The job is done and it's done right. Never no worries with Dominic. Never. Was an easy choice making him number two. He's a natural.

Goes back to when they were kids. Divvying up sides for a stickball game? Who swiped the broom from the hardware store and cut off the sweeper part? Who brought fresh vegetables to his Mom, pinching them from the wagon while the owner was upstairs making a delivery? Who broke in the back window of a store, was first to climb in and come out with some stash? Who got into the movie house and opened up the fire exit door so all the gang could sneak in free? Dominic was the one Angelo almost always chose; always eager, braver, more cold-blooded.

Angelo was at all times the one in charge, coming up with the plans, making the calls on who did what to whom and when. From the very beginning, he was the brain behind every prank or crime, and the first to punch somebody out who needed it—or worse. Like the time Louie Fagnano, from the corner building, made the mistake of late one night coming home drunk. It was Friday—payday. The boys, with their knitted stockings pulled over their faces, dragged the wine-soaked factory worker into an alley to rob him of his hard-earned money. Paisano or no paisano—he had cash, and the kids wanted it. Louie sobered up quick and brandished a push button stiletto. There were a few minor cuts to the muggers…and one major one when Angelo pulled out his own switchblade. While the rest of the gang got Louie on the ground—with a cruel smile, Angelo cut Louie's throat from one side to the other, then kicked his neighbor's face into a pulp. His first kill. There was an oath that night, a blood oath of loyalty to Angelo, to each other, and to a cruel, sadistic, bizarre and single-minded way of life that only grew in sometimes manic, yet controlled intensity as the teenagers moved on into adulthood, and to even more sordid and more violent criminal activities.

When Angelo took over the mob from Fat Frankie, the determined and ruthless new leader was the unanimous choice of all the soldiers; held in high esteem for the bold and cold way he disposed of the former boss who accidentally fell onto ambitious Angelo's open switchblade. Eight times. And for the ironical way Angelo disposed of the body; Fat Frankie was a golf nut, and appropriately buried up in the Bronx in Van Cortlandt Park, a popular public golf course, a few hours before the first group of golfers teed off. "It's the least we could do," Angelo boasted to his boyhood friends Dapper Dominic, Gino the Grip, Eddie Lump Lump, Beansey, and Rocco the Socko, all who had become the core of his organization.

"Hello gorgeous," Angelo greeted Rosie, pinching her cheek as he leaned over her desk. "You getting prettier every day. Must be all the bananas you're taking into that beautiful body."

"Oh yeah? When do I get yours, Angelo? You could go to the head of the line anytime."

"Nice offer, sweetheart. Thanks. But I don't shit where I eat. Although your offer is tempting, very tempting, thanks, but no thanks." He looked around. "Nobody here?"

"Joey's out on the dock with Freddie and Tony, and Ira's at the dentist for a cleaning."

"So maybe you and me, maybe we can talk a little, eh?"

"Sure. What's on your mind?"

"Couple of things." Pointing around the room, with an expression that asked if there were any bugs, "We safe here? I can't keep track of all the places we do business."

"Absolutely. I'm the only fly on the wall here."

"And a good fly you are, Rosie. Very dependable, which is the way it should always be, right?"

"You don't have any doubts about me, do you, Angelo?"

"Naaah. But in our work you can't be too careful. No. You can't be too careful. So, what's going on around here?"

"Not much. Just business as usual. You know the Lowensteins, they're straight arrows. Never say anything bad about anybody, never do anything wrong. Best clients you have, I'll bet. You got anything special on your mind?"

"Yeah. A few things. Namely Dominic and Tony. What do you know?"

"I heard nobody's seen Dominic, but nobody here knows nothing. They're all in the dark like you. I hope he's okay."

Why wouldn't he be?"

"I mean, well I mean nobody knows where he is. So I'm just hoping he's okay. That's all."

"He was supposed to be here the day he turned into a fucking phantom."

"Never saw him."

"He didn't call or nothing?"

"No calls, no flowers…."

"Stop the kidding, Rosie. This is serious business."

"Sorry Angelo. No, like I said, no calls or anything."

"Just Dominic never pulled anything like this. More'n just my right arm and a big earner, he's like a brother to me, and top of that I got his wife and his mom bawling tears on my stoop. This is a very sensitive issue we're talking about here that somebody's gonna be sorry for if anything bad happened."

"You think maybe the cops got him?"

"We're checking it out with some connections uptown. But so far, the cops are not involved. And none of the other families I know of. You know we're just a middle-size family working our own territory, keeping a low profile, you might say; staying out of all the Bonanno and Vinnie John Rao crap going on with the Feds and the local law and each other the newspapers are going crazy over. The others? They leave us our business and we don't try to muscle in on theirs so you don't read about us in The Mirror or The News. We got our corner of the world, they get their divvy, and it keeps us all happy. So we just take care of number one—ourselves. So let me tell you something Rosie—and you can spread this around to any interested parties; we find out if somebody did in Dominic, or hurt him any way, I mean even a hangnail, a goddamn pimple, they'll be sorry the midwife smacked 'em on the butt 'cause we'll smack 'em so hard to send 'em back where they came from. Now tell me again; you sure he was never here that day?"

"On my brother's life, Angelo, I swear I ain't seen him."

"Okay. We'll hold it at that for now. Oh yeah, your baby brother? Last I heard he's doing real good. A no-trouble con. Like a saint. He bothers nobody and nobody bothers him. He's got a nice soft job in the joint's hospital—they all love him there, and he's doing easy time. We make sure of that for you, Rosie. Easy time. Just for you. You can count on that. You know you can count on that."

"I'm sure I can, Angelo. I'm sure I can. It's good to know he's okay and you're keeping your promise."

"Hey. That's what promises are for. What do you think? I'd go back on my word? I made that promise to you on my blessed mother's life, so you know I'm good for it. And we're working hard, real hard on getting him out early. That ain't easy, but we're making some progress. I'll keep you up to date. Now, tell me about Tony. What can we expect from the bum?"

"Oh Angelo, give him a break. He's just a pug lookin' for a different life."

"He made his bed, Rosie. Nobody twisted his arm, and it's no big secret he's twisted quite a few in his day. And more. You know the family is all about blood; we work together, take care of each other, follow the rules which go back a long way. That's the way it's been. That's the way it'll always be. Don't worry; he can get out if that's what he wants. All he has to do is what he has to do. And he's free like a bird, just maybe in a bigger cage so we know where he is. But he's out, just like he wants when he does the right thing. Right now I'm just looking to get a better feel for the situation; you know anything what he's thinking."

"My guess is that he wants out bad enough and he'll do whatever he has to do. His God thing seems real and he doesn't want to do any more hurting."

"And the Lowensteins?"

"Do they have a choice?"

Angelo smiled. "Come here, Rosie."

She rose, came round to the front of her desk, standing before a smiling Angelo.

"Gimme a hug."

She reached out and hugged him, he pulled back just a bit and stared into her beautiful green eyes, his smile turning to menacing sneer, pulled her close again and whispered into her ear, "Don't ever fuck with us Rosie. I trust you up to now. You've been a good soldier. Don't fuck it up. Don't do nothing to make me hurt you; it wouldn't be pretty. You know something, you hear something, you even smell something…you say something. Capeesh?"

"Sure, Angelo. I understand. I got nothing to say right now. If I do, you'll be the first I say it to."

"Good girl. And we'll keep taking good care of your kid brother. You can count on that. No worries. None at all. We watch him like a baby. Won't be no time you two'll be playing in the schoolyard again like when you were kids." He patted her on the ass and left.

Rosie leaned against the desk…her face as white as the paper in her typewriter roller…scared as hell.

Looking at the Lowenstein brothers like they were crazy, Sammy the Spic rose from his chair in the greasy spoon café, "Me? I'm on a boat outta here. Tonight!"

"Oh no you ain't," said Freddie. "Sit down. You bug out and we're all dead people. I mean don't even think about it. You disappear and I'll track you down and do a real job on you, wherever you hole up—even the other side of the world. On the goddamn moon, if I have to."

"Santo dios. This is muy loco; craziest thing I ever

heard. They would not do this to me. Sure, I cop a few small ones off the top; everybody does. So they send Tony to push me around a little and everything goes back to the way it was. It's part of the program. The way it is. What's the big deal? Now they want to do me? You're pulling my leg, ain't ya?"

"Wish we were," said Ira. "But we gotta make this work or I don't know what."

Sweat beads formed on Sammy's brow and began dripping down his oily face. He took out his handkerchief and was dabbing away; "They really want to put me away, and take pictures? I ain't never heard of nothing like that. Take pictures? How we know it's gonna work? How I know you get me outta the fucking water? I could freeze my cojones down there."

"We make it work and we'll get you out—fast!" Ira said. "You won't even have time for your shvantz to turn blue! I promise. How do we make it work? I got a pal—a professional, he'll tell me how to make sure it all looks legit on camera. Soon as it's over, you're outta here and on a banana boat back to Havana, or wherever. I got all kinds of connections through the shipping lines. You tell me where you want to go; I'll get you there. Maybe Havana's not such a good idea what with all that Castro crap going on, but there's a million islands in the Caribbean and you can have your choice of any of them. Even Mexico or South America."

"Shit, I got a chiquita with her kid. Them, too?"

"Maybe later. They can't be in on this now. Better they believe you're at the bottom of the Hudson."

"You sure this is the only way? I don't know I can trust anybody."

"The only way we can think, and you have no choice.

You skip out and The Boys'll find you, or Freddie will. I promise you, wherever," said Joey. "The Boys gotta believe we did it their way. They gotta believe you're dead."

"Why they wanna do this? Like I said, they already sent Tony to do me a couple times. He gives me a little professional courtesy; not lay on the damage too heavy. Just some pushing around that always kept 'em happy."

""They're not happy, now. You went too far."

"How come you so sure this works?"

"Hey, as sure as anything in this farkakte world we work in. Payoffs. Beatings. Hits. All that crap going on, and all we want to do is make an honest living."

"Me, too." said Sammy.

"You? You?" a pissed off Freddie shouted. "Making book? Skimming? Dealing with The Boys? Putting your Chiquita out on the street and pimping her? And who the hell knows what else! That's an honest living?"

"Only living I know."

"You better pick another occupation in your new life. 'Cause I don't know how many lives you're gonna have left," said Joey.

"In the meantime," added Ira, "sign this paper."

"What paper?"

"The one says Tony didn't kill you and that we staged the whole thing and that…"

"You really think," asked Joey, "this'll clear us of anything? Kind of naïve, isn't it?"

"Who knows? It's all we got."

"So what's the schedule, not that I'm a hundred percent going for it?" asked Sammy, still looking for assurances as he put his signature to the paper.

"We tell The Boys we'll do it Sunday night when no

one's around. If they wanna be there. But we do a switch and do it Saturday night."

"So what do we tell The Boys after?"

"That we got word Sammy here got wind of the whole thing and was skipping town and we had to do it fast."

"Will they buy it?"

"If Joey's pictures are good enough, we might get lucky and they'll buy it."

"If they don't?"

"They'll have to. "

"This better work," pleaded Sammy. "I'm one dead Cuban it don't come off."

"Don't worry. You won't be the only corpse in the cemetery."

"One way or another Sammy, you're one dead Cuban. You cease to exist. You're kaput! Finito! No phone calls from wherever the hell you are. No letters. No telegrams. No smoke signals. No carrier pigeon. No nothing. Not even mind signals. Maybe six or nine months you have somebody—maybe a travel agency wherever you are, send a letter to our office asking if we're interested in a vacation or something and sign it Uncle Sam or whatever clues us it's you. We'll know where you are and arrange for your girlfriend and her kid—if they're still around and interested, get them down there. But it's silencio all the way, all the time. Silencio! Entindido! Understand?"

"Si. Si. I understand. But the whole fucking thing is still muy loco."

"You bet your life it is!"

10.

ACCORDING TO THE PLAN, TONY TALKED TO GINO AND AR-ranged a sit-down with Angelo. It was lunchtime at La Columba in the not-open-to-the-public back room where Tony sat across the table from the boss.

"So paisan," Angelo opened the conversation, "we got a deal? You ready to ice the Spic."

"Not somethin' I really want to do, Angelo. I ain't never..."

"I know. I know. It's just business. Strictly business."

"I do it and I'm out? Clean?"

"Clean as a new bar of Lifebuoy. We just want to know you're hanging close to the neighborhood and choosing your friends very carefully."

"That's it," asked Tony skeptically. "Nothin' else?"

"...and you're that 'clam' you keep talking about. Shut. And shut tight."

"Wasn't easy to make up my mind."

"These things? Never is. Once you do, it's a breeze. One or two bangs to Sammy's head with your Louisville, some cement blocks, a push into the Hudson, it's all over, and you're with you and your God. Whatever. Matter of fact, I'm thinking, maybe it's a good idea me or one us is on hand when you do it."

Tony swallowed hard. Now came the hard part.

"You don't trust me after all these years? You'll have the pictures."

"Nothing to do with trust. It's a matter of personal observation and verification. Yeah, that's right, seeing and believing. Capeesh? The pictures? They're the insurance."

"I wasn't thinkin' of a crowd, Angelo. This ain't Friday night at St. Nick's."

"Hey. Hey. Always a pleasure to watch a pro at work. Yeah, one of us'll be there. I think that's the way it should be. Yeah. That's what I think. Okay?"

"Not what I was thinkin', but if that's the way you see it."

"That's the way I see it. Make sure Joey is good with his camera and plenty of fresh film? Can't go and forget the film, now. Right? And the flash? Camera's got a flash, right? That's gotta work good too, you doing it at night."

"They say he's a good photographer with that heinie camera. But I don't think he ever did anythin' like this, though I heard he did see some bad things over there when he was a GI and win some medals."

"Then this'll be a piece of cake for him. Bring back some nice memories of dead Nazis. And you? You just gotta do what you gotta do. One more thing?"

"Yeah?"

"Dominic."

"Yeah, I heard. It's all over the dock. You got any news?"

"Nothing yet. You know anything? Anything at all?"

"No. I'm in the dark, like you."

"You hear something you tell me. Capeesh?"

"Sure. I hear anythin'."

"Okay. Now? Che ne dici di qualcosa da mangiare? Let's have some lunch. Vinnie makes a house special a little steak filet goes good with a side of pasta drowning in marinara—his own mother's recipe, may she rest in peace."

"Thanks, but I gotta go and make things final with the Lowensteins. You know they ain't too keen on this. They're not sure 'bout the whole thing, like me."

"But they'll do it, right?"

"Said they would. But none of us ain't relaxed with all this."

"You'll be surprised Tony. Like swinging at a Whitey Ford pitch he telegraphed you from the mound."

"Yeah, Whitey Ford—only the greatest. Like he's gonna telegraph a pitch."

"Ahhh Tony. You, you're the greatest." Angelo put his arm around his enforcer and walked him to the door leading into the restaurant. "One way or the other, you'll always be part of the family. Keep Gino posted on the big night. Remember, a couple of swings with the lumber and we're rid of a lying cheating little spic scumbag and you get a new life like you want. Ciao."

As Tony shuffled away, Angelo called out, "Hey Vinnie, medium rare. You know. The way I like."

11.

"HOW'D IT GO, TONY," IRA ANXIOUSLY ASKED.

"I think I done good. Just like you guys said. We just gotta tell Gino the night. They wanna be there."

"What they want and what we'll give them are two different things," declared Freddie. "I've had enough of these arrogant guinea bastards."

"Cool it, Freddie," urged Joey. "We still have a long way to go. And we'd better keep level heads…or we'll lose 'em."

12.

THEY WERE ALONE IN THE OFFICE, TONY AND ROSIE, AND she was standing behind him massaging his tense shoulders. "Like knots, Tony. Might take forever to work them out."

"I really appreciate this, Rosie. Ain't felt this tight since the old days when I was workin' the Friday nights inside the ropes. They say you got the touch."

"I'm sure they say a lot more. I'll bet I'm the talk of the town."

"Ahhh Rosie, nobody says bad things about you. You're a good girl. With a big heart."

"I don't know anymore. All this is taking me down. I feel like my whole world is collapsing around me. My brother probably won't live out his time. He'll do himself in before anything like that happens again. He's that kind of personality."

"Maybe he's stronger than you think."

"I hope so. And me, too. I hope I'm stronger than I'm thinking right now. All this stuff with you and the Lowensteins—I'm even wondering what kind of jerk I've been sleeping around like I do. What's the future in it for me? I'll be a grey haired old woman with wrinkled boobs down to my knees and still looking for I don't know what."

"Don't be so hard on yourself, Rosie. You ain't done no

damage to people like what I done; just givin' them lots of lovin', maybe. Nothin' too wrong with that. Patty says the world needs a lot more lovin'."

"Not the way I toss it around. I'm like a damn punch-board. A wonder I don't have bed sores."

"You know, sometimes you just gotta do what you gotta do an' get out of it what you can."

"You do a lot of talking to God?"

"Yeah. kinda helps clear my head."

"Does God tell you what to do?"

"Not really. Just lets me talk it out till I come up with an answer."

"Is it always the right answer?"

"Sometimes I think it is. And sometimes I find out it ain't. So back to talkin' it out again I go."

"You're a nice man, Tony. Patty's lucky to have you."

"I put her through a lot, you know, an' it ain't over yet. So I'm still lookin' for the right answers."

"You think the plan'll work?"

"I don't know. Guess we'll be givin' it a shot. Not much else we can do. What about you, Rosie? You stickin' around after, what with Angelo not bein' straight with you on your brother?"

"Where would I go? "

"Away from here, maybe where the sun is shinin'…."

"Yeah, maybe where the sun is shining. That's something to think about. How's the neck feeling?"

"Hey, you're good! You could open up a shop."

"That's an idea. Maybe I'll do just that. Where the sun is shining."

13.

ARMED WITH A FEW TIPS FROM HIS SHOW BIZ NEIGHBOR, Ira laid out the plan to his brothers and Tony, one more time.

"Tony, you bring Sammy to the pier about ten o'clock Saturday night. Freddie and me, we'll bring the ketchup, the blankets, the cement blocks, and the ropes. Don't forget the bat. Sammy's gonna be one scared rabbit, so you gotta keep assuring him we'll get him out of the water quick. If he gives you any hard time, you got my permission to cold cock him. Whichever, on the dock we leave him standing, tie him up with the rope, but real loose-like, no knots. His legs and his arms, so he can get out easy after he hits the water. Now to the Hollywood stuff. My neighbor says when you swing the bat swing it right in front of his face so you just miss him. Measure good in a practice swing. And the real one you swing with all your might like DiMaggio, so it looks like you mean business. Like I said, measure it good first so you know you'll miss him. He says in the picture it'll look like you're going right for his head. Sammy'll cringe or flinch natural. Joey'll catch the picture as you're swinging just before the bat passes Sammy's head. May have to do it a couple of times. Next picture? You place the bat against the side of Sammy's head—press hard so it looks like you connected. I'll bet Sammy'll make a face looks like he's getting smacked, and Joey'll take another picture. But we may not need this shot if it don't come out realistic. Then we lay him on the ground and cover the side of his head with the ketchup and put some on the bat and that's another shot. The cement blocks? You know what? Let's forget about it—it'll only freak out Sammy more. I got a better idea. Tony, you just roll him off the dock and forget about the blocks and Joey gets a picture of him going off or maybe hitting the water, too. We fish him out quick-like, and we're out of there."

"What'll The Boys think without the blocks?"

"I don't know. Tony can tell 'em we panicked and were anxious to get rid of the body fast. Maybe that one of the dock security was coming around."

"Still sounds crazy."

"Got another idea?"

"No."

"Okay with you, Tony?"

"You guys are the smart ones. I'm just the muscle."

14.

"I GOTTA TELL YOU SOMETHING," FREDDIE SAID, SITTING opposite his brothers in the booth at the greasy spoon diner across from the office. "We always level with each other, right? The Lowensteins—three meshuginah brothers taking a gamble in the crazy banana shipping business and making it work. I'm really proud of us. We did good. Ma would be proud of us. But I think I fucked up. I mean really fucked up."

"Can't be that serious…can it?"

"Yeah. Serious. Real serious."

"Okay already. What'd you do?"

"It was me. It was me done in Dominic.

"What?"

"He's dead."

"Oh no," cried Ira. "You didn't."

"Couldn't help it. The shmuck came at me with a knife. Said he'd hurt our deal with Avery, and he called me a kike."

"That sonovabitch. Did you have to kill him?"

"It was an accident. I swear it.""

"Oh man, are we in deep dreck."

"I told you. It was an accident. I slugged him and he tripped and fell in the river. It was just automatic…I wasn't even thinking. Like I was back fighting the Nips again. He made threats. I only did what came natural."

"Are you okay?"

"Yeah, I'm alright. Just glad to get it off my chest. Don't like holding things back from you two."

"Anybody else know?"

"Rosie. Only Rosie. But she's good with it, she can keep it quiet."

"We better hope so."

"What do we do now?"

"Just go on like normal, after we finish this other farka-kte piece of business."

"Normal? I ain't seen normal since Tony told us he wanted out."

"Oy, oy, oy!" groaned Ira. "Why is my heart beating like it's being played by Gene Krupa?"

"Let's do what we can to keep it beating."

"I'm with you. So are we ready? Tony should be delivering Sammy anytime now. Let's get everything out to the pier."

15.

SO FAR SO GOOD. TONY WAS COMING DOWN THE PIER WITH Sammy still complaining this stupid plan might not work, and in his doubt making half-hearted efforts to hold back. Tony poked him with the bat to keep him moving. It was cold, but not that usual Hudson River wintertime night-time bitterness. No sleet or snow or wind, only a full moon incongruously reflecting romantically on the scattered ice floes floating in the river, putting light to the scene. A murder was being faked. A business was trying to survive. A cast of characters was trying to fool people who made their living fooling people. And here was this beautiful lovers' moon. Talk about the absurd.

Joey had his Leica loaded with Agfapan 100 black and white film, what the pro at the photography shop recommended. "German film for a German camera." Perched on a tripod, the camera was attached by a coiled cable to a supplemental flash over which Joey had placed a piece of gauze to soften the lighting. Joey knew what he was do-ing, having taken a night course at the local high school. The pictures would be good. They'd be better if there's any decent acting, he thought. But that's why there's a lot of film—keep shooting till it's right. "My God," he thought, "I'm treating this like I'm taking pictures at my kid's birth-day party."

Sammy was crying; "How do I trust you guys? How do I trust you don't lemme drown?"

"Look, look, stupid, there's a rope here tied to the cleat. Look down, whaddya see?"

Sammy peered over the edge. "Is that a life preserver?"

"Right, and there's another one right here. You go in, Joey takes a picture of you hitting the water, the ropes come off easy, and you make for the one down there. We'll also toss this one next to you, too. We'll get you out. We ain't murderers. Even got a couple of blankets, and here in my pocket a flask of rum so you don't freeze your cajones you're so worried about. Shoulda been worried about 'em when you were taking money from The Boys off the top."

"Hey. I don't need you lecturing me. I know my business."

"Considering why we're all here and what we're doing, I don't think so. But you better hope we know ours. Let's get this show on the road. You ready, Joey?"

"I guess so. Do the ropes, Tony. I'll get a couple shots. Just lemme load my pocket with more bulbs—I got extras right here in the bag.

"Remember," cried Sammy. "Loose, Tony! Keep them knots fuckin' loose!"

"I ain't stupid, Sammy. I remember things. You think I want you on my conscience, too?"

"I don't make it outta this, I want to be on everybody's conscience. I'm countin' on you guys."

"Just shut up and let Tony finish with the ropes. Good thing is at least you don't have to act like you're mad."

They were all involved in their respective roles when Angelo suddenly appeared from behind a nearby stack of oil drums, pulling Rosie behind him and calling out,

"Well Tony, looks like you brought the whole Lowenstein family. Who's watchin' the store?"

In one hand a pistol. An automatic. The other gripped tightly over Rosie's wrist. "It ain't Rosie," he snarled.

Rosie? Blood was caked under her nostrils. One eye was closed, puffed up like she'd gone three rounds in the ring with Tony. She was sobbing. "I'm sorry, Tony. I'm sorry, Freddie. I'm really sorry."

"Holy shit, Angelo, what'd you do?" cried Freddie. "She's just a girl."

"Ahhh, you Lowenstein jerks. Trying to fake us out… we been doing this kind of stuff before you were born. You can't fool the foolers. Faking it with Sammy? Drowning my goombah? Naah, we do this stuff in our sleep. You can't get up early enough in the morning."

"We're just trying to save a life, here, Angelo." Ira called out.

"So what about Dominic, eh? You didn't save his life. What'd you do that for, Freddie? Couldn't just talk out the problem with him?"

"The galoot pulled a knife on me."

"So what's a little knife? He wouldn't o' hurt you. Probably just trying to make a point. Just doing a little business. You never should have killed him."

"It was an accident, but he got what he asked for, for chrissakes. What about Rosie, did you have to beat her up?" Freddie shouted.

"Still got the hots for Miss Round-heels, Freddie? This punta ain't so pretty now, is she? And she'll do or say anything to save her stinky fucked up little brother. Even rat on you lying Jews and Tony the punch-drunk moron. And don't think of trying anything. None of you. She's the first to go, and my friend Gino—come on out Gino, he's got a sawed off that'll take a couple of you out all the same time. Forget about trying anything. Even thinking about it."

Angelo wasn't kidding. A smiling Gino slipped out from behind the oil drums holding a nasty looking double-barreled sawed off shotgun pointed right at the group. "I buoni amici di sera, good evening friends," Gino announced.

I told ya this wouldn't work," cried Sammy. "I told you."

"Shut up you fucking piece of vomit," Angelo shouted, and turned to the brothers; "We always warned you that we know everything. Or can find things out. I thought you Jews were supposed to be smart."

"Come on, Angelo," implored Tony. "They was just tryin' to help me out. A lot more than you my family, a lot more than you. An' I ain't no moron. You should be ashamed."

"Don't talk about ashamed, Tony. Not to me. I know all you done over these years. I know how many arms you broke. Knees. Ribs. I know how many you put in the hospital. Don't talk to me about being ashamed. You're the rat. You're the traitor. You're the one turned away from your family."

"I shoulda done it a long time ago. You guys ain't family. Talk about fakin' here? You're the fakes. You kill your own. An' somebody axes one like Dominic you say it ain't fair. You don't know fair. You didn't even treat me fair when I was in the ring takin' dives, outclassed, an' gettin' butchered."

"You finished, Tony? 'Cause this party's gonna be over."

"No, I'm not finished."

"Save it, Tony," said Joey down on one knee near his camera bag. "These guys'll never change, whatever you say."

"Hey. Hey. Hey. Put the guns down," pleaded Sammy. "I give all the money back, I swear. All of it. Even more on top. I got a little stashed away. It's all yours. Honest. All of it."

"Stai zitto tu puzzolente ladeo poco. Shut up you stinking little thief. You're the cause of a lot of this anyway." Angelo shouted. "It'll be a special pleasure doing you in. And it won't be fake. I got more news for all of you. We finish here, Tony's family goes down—we take care of Patty and the kid, just like Freddie took one of my family down. Una via per una vita. Una morte per una morte. À life for a life. A death for a death!"

Tony, still with the bat in his hand, cried from deep inside, "No. You won't. You won't. You can't. They got nothin' to do with this. I'll kill you first."

"Oh, you're gonna kill me, eh? Whatever happened to all that bullshit about you and your God? Tony, Tony… you're a phony. Hey, Tony the Phony. Look at me, I'm a poet."

"Ain't enough bullets gonna stop me from puttin' this bat to you, Angelo. Before I die you're a dead man, too. I swear to God, may he forgive me. You leave my Patty an' little Tony alone. They ain't done nothin' to you."

Joey, who'd been getting flashbulbs out of the bag on the ground next to the tripod, drew his hand quietly out of the bag. As he had learned in Army Ranger training, and cultivated in bloody and fatal hand-to-hand combat against the German enemy, he rolled over, quickly and expertly fired the Luger. Once. Twice. The first bullet smashing Gino right between the eyes, with the sawed-off firing harmlessly into the air as he fell. The second hitting Angelo in the shoulder, causing him to drop the pistol and release his hold on Rosie. Snarling in pain and anger, he made an attempt to reach down to retrieve the weapon. Tony, with a feral growl, was on him in a flash, and Angelo was on the receiving end of what Sammy was supposed to get. Only this time for real—a Louisville bat crushing the side of his head. Angelo D'Alessandro fell back against an oil drum and slid down to the dock—one dead gangster boss. One dead old neighborhood paisano.

Rosie was on her knees sobbing. Tony stood over Angelo, breathing hard. Wide-eyed Ira was staring at Joey with great wonderment, and Sammy was frantically unwrapping the ropes and freaking out. Freddie was racing over to Rosie.

"Joey," said Ira. "What the hell was that?"

"My Luger," said Joey. "The camera wasn't the only thing I picked up from that dead Nazi bastard. I was just hoping I didn't forget how."

"We never knew. Now I see why Momma liked you best.""

"Thanks Joey," Tony was extending his hand for a shake. "You did good. Thank God it's over."

"I don't know if it's over." said Ira as he knelt next to Rosie, "Rosie, tell me, did Angelo have time to tell anybody, call anybody, say they were coming out here?"

"I don't know. I may have passed out for a moment, but I don't think so. They came to my apartment, he and Gino, and right away started punching me around. Said they smelled something going on and said they knew I knew what was happening. I guess you can't con the conners. They were gonna shove a…never mind, but that, and they said my brother was a dead man I didn't tell them what you guys were all up to. I could take the beating. But I couldn't let them hurt my baby brother any more. I just couldn't. I'm sorry. I'm so sorry."

"We'd a probably done the same. Don't blame yourself for anything. Just try to remember if at any time they let somebody know where they was headed."

"I don't think so. No. I wasn't out for that long. We got right into the car and came right here. Angelo was pissed. I'd never seen him so mad. We going to be okay? They coulda told somebody before. Are we going to be okay?"

"Okay? Well, I think you're out of a job, unless we can get Avery to make the deal right away and they keep you on. Can't worry about all that now. Chances are good somebody knew. They'll either be after us or they won't. We just all gotta be prepared both ways.

"Well," said Rosie, "I didn't want to be in the banana business any more."

"We neither, right boys?" Ira asked his brothers. "I think we're out, too. Between our investments and if we can peddle our customer list and company good will fast, we'll be okay. Not as good as maybe we waited another couple of years, but for sure we won't starve. What about you, Tony? Looks like you're out like you wanted…but there's probably a lot of undone business."

"I don't know. I gotta talk to Patty. I got a feelin' no matter what, we're gonna talk about movin' somewhere. I don't like Patty an' little Tony livin' with anythin' hangin' over. A guy I used to be in the ring with, he's got a small boxin' club an' gym in Seattle, always been askin' me to move out an' be a partner. Teachin' kids, cardin' a few smokers, workin' some new guys inna bein' contenders, gettin' fat people back in shape—maybe I wasn't much of champ in the ring, but I learned a few things I didn't forget. Now might be the right time. Get far away from here. I got a lot of talkin' to do with God…"

"You know," offered Ira, "with the Feds and the D.A.

starting to come in and clean up the docks, a bunch of the heavies already up on indictments, and a lot of them killing each other off who they think are going blab to the Grand Jury or muscling in on their territories, maybe they all got bigger fish to fry than coming after us."

"From your lips to the banana god's ears."

"Hard to say, but it would be good."

"Anyway, I suppose," added Ira, "that if we dump these bodies in the river and let 'em go find Dominic, we can always claim we never saw 'em. Or tell 'em we heard rumors about Bonanno not happy with their working arrangements and word was he was gunning for them. Last, we tell 'em Sammy skipped town, right Sammy? You're gone, right?"

"You betcha I'm gone. I don't want no part of these banditos no more. They don't play fair. Or you guys either."

"Let's clean up this mess and get out of here."

"Good idea. Don't forget their guns. Throw 'em far out. The Luger too, Joey. Makes no sense keeping that around now."

"I think I might hold on. We're not out of this yet. I'll stow it some place nobody'll know. Been able to keep it secret so far."

"True. You managed to hide it okay all these years. Some brother you are," said Freddie. "Never knew you had it. For the rest of this, maybe we'll get lucky and be okay. We'll just have to take it one day at a time. First, we have to get Rosie to Doc Tripler—he's one of the good guys; he won't say anything or file a report."

Sammy? Still shaking, still complaining. "You guys. You coulda had me killed. You're all mucho loco. I'm outta here. You guys are memories!"

"Hey! The feeling's mutual. Hasta la vista."

Walking fast, almost a trot, back toward the terminal, Sammy spun around shouting, "You're all mucho loco. This whole fuckin' thing was mucho loco." And he was gone, disappearing into the darkness as a drifting blue-gray cloud moved over to hide the moon.

"Yeah," said Tony. "Mucho loco. It's a crazy world. But it's the only one we got, thank God. I'll tell you this, it's a lot more than this punched out muscle-head can handle. Joey. Ira. Freddie. You too. Rosie. You're all good people. woulda worked out nice bein' together. I'd a liked that. Maybe we'll see each other again. Right now I gotta get home to Patty. She worries when I'm out. She's a nice lady, best thing ever happened to me. Oh yeah, Joey..." as he tied the cement blocks to Angelo's legs, slid them over the edge of the pier and watched their weight pull the body over and down into the Hudson below, "I remember you told me Dominic said to you one time?"

"What's that?"

'This river, it washes away a lot of troubles?'

Then, Tony picked up the Louisville Slugger, took one last look at it, and heaved that scarred bat of a thousand sordid stories into the Hudson River—far as he could.

The bat took one bounce off a chunk of floating ice, breaking the floe in two...then *splash*.

EPILOGUE

AS QUICKLY AS THEY COULD MAKE THE ARRANGEMENTS, they all removed themselves from the city itself…moving as far away as they felt comfortable. Felt safe. But never stopped looking over their shoulders, knowing The Boys have long memories and long reaches. It's a helluva way to live, but at least—for now, they're still living. Some of them.

Sammy the Spic?

Made a lot of money—and a lot of women, on cruise ships sailing out of Nassau. There was always a rich widow to seduce and scam, or a vacationing horny schoolteacher or secretary to bed. Sammy's mistake was hitting on a South American beauty with a bagful of cash whose husband turned out to be a Columbian drug lord. Her two nasty bodyguards, who accompanied the bride wherever she traveled, turned Sammy into shark bait somewhere off the Abacos.

Freddie?

After Avery Freight bought JIF, and after their divorce, Fran went back to her pre-married name and Freddie moved to St. John in the U.S. Virgin Islands. Leaving his sons? That was the hardest part. But they were safer away from him. The buyout was good…might have been better and more lucrative waiting a little longer, but the brothers were anxious to move out and on. Even so, there was plenty to divvy up, and they'd had enough of The Boys and all the New York and dock meshiga (craziness). For Freddie, enough for a generous settlement with Fran, and to disappear. He opened a fishing charter business on St. John that was doing well, especially considering the location was one of the top fishing grounds in the world. Freddie offered half-day, full-day, ¾-day trips, providing the tackle, bait, ice and beverages. Fishermen came from all over looking for Marlin, Dorado, Tuna, Wahoo, Snapper, King Fish, Skip Jacks and more. Whether a novice or a seasoned pro, Freddie'd take them out in his new 33-foot diesel powered sport fishing boat and gave them each a Caribbean fishing experience to remember.

And there was the freedom from Fran's compulsive neatness. Although, she'd trained him well—he kept his boat trim and shipshape.

Freddie's charter fishing career—and more, ended in a moment of sheer serendipity, when a vacationer from up north, strolling the dock looking to charter a fishing trip, caught the name on Freddie's boat. The vacationer? Eddie Lump Lump.

The explosion blew Gefilte Fish II to pieces. Freddie, too.

Joey?

He changed his name, shaved his head, grew a beard, and moved out to Long Island's Hamptons where he opened a little garage servicing European and exotic cars. His timing was impeccable

With some Hamptonites tracing family history back ten to twelve generations, many of New York City's new moneyed elite—a growing group of movers and shakers, began fast buying up some of this historic area's beautiful old properties, restoring, or building traditional and modern manors. Bringing along their Porsches, Maseratis, Ferraris, Jags and Bentleys, that inevitably required the deft touch of the master craftsman Joey had become.

While Joey and his family don't get involved in the social life and municipal politics of this year-round paradise, they do enjoy the carefree, vacation-like atmosphere, charming New England-type villages and faultless beaches.

"We keep a low profile," he wrote to Ira. "It's safer that way."

The Luger stays hidden under his bed.

Ira?

He and Bea moved to Europe. To Paris. Far enough away from The Boys (not to say France doesn't have it's own organized criminal elements), but plenty of distance from his old stateside nemeses. With enough theater and opera and restaurants in the City of Lights, as well as short train rides to other European capitols, towns and villages to satisfy their esthetic and bon vivant appetites. Together, using Bea's maiden name as the author, they're writing a book; "An American's Guide to the European Good Life." Bea had majored in the Classics and English at Manhattan's Hunter College and always wanted to be a writer. With her talent and Ira's financial and moral support… why not? Vive la belle vie.

Rosie?

Under the gentle care of Doctor Sam Tripler, Rosie recuperated from the beating, and fell deeply in love with the handsome middle-aged Doctor in the process. The feeling was mutual. They married and moved upstate where Sam opened a clinic. Rosie never did shake off her nymphomania, but that was all right with Sam who capably handled Rosie's avaricious sexual cravings to both their satisfactions. Also, Rosie began providing therapeutic massage services to Sam's patients, which was a bad thing…and a good thing. The hands-on treatments with male patients (and a few attractive female ones, too), stirred old feelings—some yearnings, in Rosie's loins. But she had become strong enough to be able to stow them in a "safe box"—to which only Sam had the key.

What happened to her brother? Nobody knows. If anyone does, they don't talk about it.

Tony?

Intent on leaving the City and everything behind, he made contact with Izzy Pearlman who was an expert in providing new I.D. to people who had the need and the money to pay. Some dead person's inactive, yet still valid social security number, driver's license, passport—whatever. Izzy could even recommend a surgeon who disguised fingerprints, and did full face jobs.

Armed with new papers, Tony, Patty and little Tony moved west to Seattle and joined up with his old ring buddy who ran the gym he'd often talked about. Tony stayed in the background, putting a few bucks into the setup to bring the facilities up to date, and things were going good. They had a some young up-and-comers training, ran a teen club that helped keep kids off the streets, set up a corner of the gym for body builders, and were working on initiating open-to-the-public aerobics programs.

Tony was never happier. Things were going well. He was still talking to God every day, and his heart would get lighter each time he unburdened. Most nights he even slept well. There were the other nights…

"Tony! Tony! Wake up. Wake up." You're having a nightmare."

His pajamas soaked from perspiration, Tony sat up in the bed.

"Are you all right," his wife asked, turning on the bed lamp.

"Okay. Okay. I'm okay." He managed to say while catching his breath.

"What in heavens name were you dreaming. You were punching the air like a madman."

"It was awful, Patty. Awful. I was at the gym thinkin' how great things were; the partnership here, little Tony not so little anymore an' likin' it out here. You more beautiful than ever. That the docks an' everythin' are 3000 miles away… an' all of a sudden somebody taps me on the shoulder. I turn around. I don't know this guy, just he's a paisan an' there's somethin' about him—a look, a look that's familiar. From the old days. It's what he said made me start swingin'. I'm sorry honey. I didn't mean to scare you."

"What'd he say made you so angry?"

"He said the same old things, "You got a nice operation here, Tony. Be a pity something bad happened. My friends an' me, we can make sure nothin' bad happens. With us, you spend a little money to save a lot of money…an' you won't have no trouble."

"So I started swingin'…I was wishin' I had my old Louisville."

"Oh Tony, you're still shaking. That's an ugly nightmare; but just a nightmare. The one we lived through, the real nightmare, that's over. Been a couple of years and we haven't heard anything. Nothing. Been a long time. Come here. Let me hug you. We're okay. We're okay now. I told you not to eat that cold pizza before you went to bed. Go back to sleep. We're going to be okay. You can talk to God about it in the morning."

Patty switched off the bed lamp. Lying there in the dark she couldn't help but wonder…just how far away is yesterday? How deep is the bottom of the river?

ACKNOWLEDGMENTS

MY GRATITUDE TO: DR. SCHWEITZER, SENSITIVE AND KIND English teacher at William Howard Taft High School in the Bronx, for his encouragement. The U.S. Navy where I learned what I wanted to do for the rest of my life. My U.S. Marine brothers who often saved my life. Henry Ford II for whom I wrote my first ad. Every advertising agency executive and client who blue-penciled my work whether it made sense or not. It made me smarter and tougher. Brian Hamilton, editor and friend. And thanks to Gilles Comeau for his brilliant contribution to the cover design. My mom and dad for that Corona-Smith typewriter when I was twelve years old…and their love. My baby brother, Jordan, for brightening my life. My son, Seth, and my dear wife, Shirley, who live on in my heart. And my daughter, Alison, who is every father's dream.

We are the sum of the people in our lives and of our experiences. I am one fortunate man.

GROWING UP ON THE STREETS OF NEW YORK CITY, ED GRUBER became a U.S. Navy Journalist writing and producing radio programs and films for the Pacific Command Public Information Office. As a Combat Correspondent, Ed served on board aircraft carriers, destroyers and a submarine, and with Marine Corps infantrymen on combat night patrols. After his distinguished military service, he had a long and prolific career serving world-class clients as a writer and creative director with international advertising agencies in New York, Detroit and Toronto, and as a freelance writer and marketing consultant. Ed wrote newspaper, magazine, and outdoor ads, radio and television commercials, executive speeches, and created motivational corporate films that he produced in Hollywood and Toronto studios. He is a widower, currently residing in Woodstock Georgia.